UNSTEADY LOVE FROM A THUG

KYEATE

Unsteady Love from A Thug

Unsteady Love from A Thug Copyright 2019 by Kyeate

Published by Mz. Lady P Presents, LLC

All rights reserved

STAY CONNECTED

SYNOPSIS

Meet Eze Sadiq, ruthless, cold and intimidating are just a few words to describe him. Growing up, life dealt Eze a bad hand, which caused him to direct his pain in other forms. Despite growing up in the gritty streets of Nashville, Eze built his empire by running an underground female fight club.

Life isn't always unicorns and rainbows which SunJai Perkins knows that all too well. Never imagining life could be so bad, SunJai finds herself in one of the worse places imaginable. After being sold to Eze and being placed on his team, SunJai finds herself fighting for her life, literally and figuratively.

SunJai's timid and innocent ways catch Eze's eye and he goes against his code. However, underlining issues from his past has caused him not to love another.

Despite the undeniable chemistry between the pair, Eze's hearts remain ice cold towards SunJai.

When a surprising matter knocks on SunJai's door, she must work towards sparing her heart and gaining her freedom.

Follow Eze and SunJai as they embark on a journey of secrets, lust, and loyalty. Find out what it truly means to have unsteady love from a thug.

A WHOLE LOTTA GANG SHHH

As I am writing this, my eyes are droopy, my back hurts, and my hair is a mess, but I said let me speak to a few folks because I had stopped writing this part of the book so many books ago. When I started this book, the second day of writing, I was hit with a huge test that required extra dedication and extra work. I was told I could no longer write on my day job. I used to write during break and naptime because I'm a teacher, and I have written most of my entire catalog at work. That meant when I got home, less time focusing on my kids and longer nights in which now I'm tired at my day job from the night before, but I did it.

I want to thank my coworkers and supporters Diamond, Fran, Cae Cae, and Neshia. Gang Gang! My Fab 5 Ariel, La'Nisha, Tip Montana, C. Michelle. These girls have been a huge help, not just to me, but to each other as well. I love y'all.

To my children, especially Zion Makenzie, this go around you were my Zen. When I told you about the situation at my job, you told me what to come home and do so that I can focus as I do at work. While locked in my room, when I was thirsty, you made sure I was straight, and when I wasn't eating, you were bringing me a bowl of noodles. Before bed, you would ask if I had met my goal, and I thank you for staying on me.

My publisher Mz. Lady P, I can't thank you enough for being the absolute best, trustworthy, honest, and real. With the mess going on within the industry right now, I couldn't be prouder to be a part of MLLP. Thank you again.

My readers old and new I thank you for rocking with me and being patient. I'm so thankful for the continual support and thank you for letting me be your favorite author.

ONE

EZE (EASY) SADIQ

"Yes, Eze!" ole girl called out as I hit her with full force long deep strokes. With each thrust, she was throwing that ass back. Sweat dripped from my chest, falling onto her back. It was hot as a bitch in here, and I was trying like hell not to succumb to my death while trying to catch a nut.

"Fuck me, baby!" she screamed.

I ain't have time for all this theatric shit, and I wasn't a talker during sex. All I needed was something warm to catch this nut, and then I'm gone. Using my free hand, I reached forward and grabbed her hair, wrapping my hand in her hair.

"Damn Eze, don't pull too hard. This is a wig," she complained.

Irritated off that shit alone, I used my hand and shoved her head forward, pressing that shit into the mattress. With both hands on her hips, I closed my eyes and continued stroking. I had to get this shit up out of me and fast. Time was cutting it close. My phone dinged, which was on the nightstand, so I looked down at my watch, and the text I was waiting on came through.

"Catch this shit," I demanded while pulling my dick out.

While she turned around towards me, I snatched the condom off. She was ready too, tongue all out, holding her breast. All I could do was smirk at the thought that popped in my head. In one quick motion, I yanked her wig off her head and nutted on her Cleo's.

"What the fuck, Eze?" she yelled, and I placed the wig back on top of her head.

"I was just making sure your wig was secured," I laughed and took off towards the bathroom. I know I wasn't shit, and nobody needed to tell me what I already knew.

As soon as I got in the bathroom, I looked around in the closet for a clean rag. Grabbing some soap, I cleaned my dick off getting it back fresh. Looking in the mirror, I grinned and ran my tongue across my gold teeth. With no time to waste, I headed back out to the bedroom to get my shit because I had to bounce. She was so pissed at my ass that she ain't even look my way.

"Aite, then I holla at ya," I said before exiting the room.

"Eze, you not gone give me no money for my hair? That shit was trifling." She pouted.

"That shit will wash out, girl. You done caught my nut in far worse places. I got to go. I got you next time." I hit her with the deuce and headed out.

When stepping outside, I pulled my hoodie over my head and hit the remote start on my truck. It was cold as hell out here, and I left my coat in the truck. I didn't have time taking all my shit in gal's house. As soon as I got in the truck, I placed my hands together and blew into them. After a few minutes, I pulled my phone out to get the address off the text that had come to my phone. It was time to go to work.

Most people would look down on my job description,

but it had me eating well. At twenty-five, I wasn't your average street nigga. Hell, I probably was worse depending on how you look at it. I wasn't into selling drugs. I used my gift of hands differently. Pulling off, I headed to the secret location of today's job.

Life for me consisted of one thing, and that was money. Money was the only thing I could possess that I controlled. It didn't hurt me, and it didn't betray me like the average human. Now money can make people do those things, but I didn't have that problem because nobody got close enough to harm me in that way. It was only me out here. A nigga wasn't in a relationship, had no children, and no family. I had one nigga that was my right hand, and that was it.

Pulling up at the location, I cut the engine and peeped the scene. The lot was full, so I knew it was about to be a big money night. That shit made my dick hard thinking of the cash out at the end of the night. Reaching into the glove box, I pulled out my brush and went over my waves a few times. Tossing it back in the box, I got out and headed to the money.

Walking into the building, it was already live, and shit ain't even started yet. Scanning the place, I was just peeping the scene and the faces. Mostly everyone there was regulars.

"Bossman!" I heard, and I turned around. It was my right-hand man, Bullet.

"How we looking?" I flat out asked.

"Shit's looking good. The new girls Diego sent are all lined up in the back," he answered. I nodded my head and followed him.

We walked through the crowd and into a sealed-off room. Entering the room, all the chatter stopped, and all eyes were on me.

"Y'all line up and face him!" Bullet demanded. It was

four girls, and they all did as they were told with frightened looks on their faces.

"Diego said these three are worth every penny you paid for. Now this one, Diego said he threw her in because she just had to go, and he hopes like hell you could do something with her." Bullet laughed his ugly ass laugh.

I glanced up at the girl that he was talking about, and she looked innocent and out of place. Directing my focus back on all of them, I crossed my arms and rubbed my facial hairs.

"Who in here knows how to fight?" I asked. They all looked at each other crazy, but nobody said anything.

"That was a motherfucking question!" I yelled.

My eyes landed on a thick, chocolate chick. She had attitude all over her. Walking up to her face, she gave me that look that most chicks gave me when they wanted dick dropped off in them.

"Can you fight?"

"I-I mean I can do a little something," she stuttered.

"You up first, but let me tell you something. This fight is one for your freedom. You can either make me some money or cause me to lose some money. I suggest you make me some because if you lose my money. You'll work that shit off until I get it back. Diego ain't sent you over here for nothing!" I spat and stepped back.

"As for the rest of you, I suggest you sit back and watch because you all gone get in the ring before the night over with. Bullet, take them to the box so they can watch and you 'Ms. I can do a little something' bring your ass!" I snapped and made my way back out to the front, where the crowd was ready for the first match.

Growing up, I stayed fighting. I could break every bone in a nigga's face with my bare hands. I had to find a way to direct my pain, and fighting was my passion, so I turned that shit into a profit by starting an underground female fight club. That was the best shit I ever did. It was hard to find females to fight, so I would cop them from this Mexican cat, Diego. Diego was into some other shit. I knew he was into trafficking girls, so for a price, he would send me special ones.

A lot of girls that came through here, I would let go, and a lot once they saw the amount of money they were bringing in would leave but remained fighters for me. I was all about the money, so I didn't care what lives they had before me or after. Hell, all I kept up with was the names and the amount of money they were making me. To make things better, I trained majority of the females to be some lethal heavy hitters.

My fight club was special invite-only, and every fight night I would have damn near two hundred spectators. Thursdays-Saturdays were fight nights, and nobody knew the location until an hour beforehand.

My folks paid a hundred dollars a pop to see a fight, so you do the math on how much I was bringing in a night. That doesn't even include bets and wagers on the girls.

Making my way up to the ring, I held the rope so that gal could get in. If she wasn't scared before, she looked that way now.

"Aite motherfuckers, put your money where your mouth is, we got a newcomer tonight!" I roared, and everybody started yelling and barking. The adrenaline that gave me was everything. It was fight night and money to be made.

TWO

EZE

We were on the last fight, and Diego was right. The other three girls that he sent had hands, especially Mocha, the first chick that got in the ring. With a little more work, she was gone be a guaranteed beast. I could tell with how she looked at a nigga she had other motives as well, but I wasn't fucking with it.

I gave Bullet the head nod for him to send the last girl up here. He gave her a shove, and she stumbled on stage. I shook my head because I knew she was about to cost me some money. Once we locked eyes, I couldn't help but peep how fine she really was.

One thing about it I could tell that shorty was not entirely black. Now when a motherfucker saw me, they loved to say something about my black ass because I was dark as hell. Shorty, even though she looked innocent, had an aura about her that didn't scream innocent. I think it was the exotic, squinty eyes she had. She looked like she was half Korean mixed with a dash of black. Her hair was all over her head, but I could tell she had some good shit, even with it being dry as fuck. All kinds of shit went through my head, and that shit was nasty as hell.

"You ready?" I asked, getting back to the mission at hand.

Damn, I hated to let her fight because she looked like a damn model in the face, and I already knew her opponent wasn't gone go easy on her.

"I don't have a choice." She shrugged.

"Look, protect your face, and think about the consequences you have to face if you cost me money. What's your name?" I asked.

"SunJai," she mumbled as I pushed her to the center.

"Aite, place your bets. Sun versus Midnight is up next!"

I stepped out the way as both of the girls took center stage. My eyes roamed over shorty's body, and she had on a pair of sweatpants and a wife beater. I could tell she was blessed in the bottom area just based on how the pants fit her frame.

Standing off in the corner, I crossed my arms as the bell dinged, and they went at it. Midnight was coming at SunJai hard, but she was blocking all her hits. I was getting pissed off because she wasn't even trying to hit Midnight. She was just protecting herself.

"Come on, man. Throw a fucking punch, Sun!" I yelled, and I don't even do that shit.

Bullet looked at me, and I pretended as if I didn't even see him. Sun was getting tired, and Midnight speed was a force. In one swift motion, Midnight threw a right hand that sent Sun flying back towards me. Sun had given up and hit the mat in defeat. Biting my bottom lip in frustration, I was mad as hell, but I knew she wasn't about to win this shit.

"TAKE THE GIRLS TO THE CRIB," I told Bullet. I was gone handle they ass a little later.

After the fight and all the payouts were done, I sat in the back and watched as they broke down the mats and shit. I ain't have nowhere to be, so I wasn't in a hurry to leave. For some wild reason, Sun kept popping up in my head. I done gave her a whole nickname out here. What piqued my interest was how in the hell she ended up with Diego's ass. I never had a reason to really question him because he was known all around because his shit was huge as hell. More than likely, she probably wasn't even from here. Me though, I was born and raised in the city. I never even thought about leaving.

Looking down at my watch, it was going on two in the morning. Standing up, I stretched and headed out of the warehouse. I needed to stop by the girls' crib before I headed home. I made sure the girls stayed in a decent place and made sure they had food, clothes, and shit, but that was it. They made they own money and were able to take care of they own needs.

As soon as I got in the truck, I headed straight there. I knew Bullet was there. That nigga had his own room in that bitch with his freaky ass. Plus, as stated, he was my right hand, and I didn't trust everyone to watch the girls.

About twenty minutes later, I pulled in the driveway behind Bullet's truck and hopped out. Using my key, I walked up the steps and let myself in the house. The house was pitched black, so I headed on down the hall until I heard something fall in the kitchen. Looking back over my shoulder, I slowly turned around and made my way back.

I could hear what sounded like whimpers, so I knew it had to be a female. When I hit the light in the kitchen, Sun stood there in shock. Her face was stained in tears, and she held a bag of ice in her hand.

"The hell are you in here crying for?" I asked. Seeing Sun cry pissed me off for some reason. Hell, I don't even know why the fuck I was mad.

"No reason, I was just getting some ice. I'll go back to my room," she stumbled over her words and tried to pass me, but I held my arm out to stop her.

Using my hand, I lifted her chin to get a good look at her eye, and she flinched.

"Girl ain't nobody about to touch your timid ass. Sit the fuck down," I ordered. She nodded quickly and took a seat at the table while I fully entered the kitchen and grabbed me a beer.

"You drink?" I asked before I sat down.

"I need something way stronger than a beer," she mumbled, holding the ice to her face.

Nodding my head, I grabbed the bottle of Hennessey from the cabinet and placed it on the table with a cup. Taking my seat across from her, she just sat there. She looked at me then down at the bottle. Taking a swig of my beer, I leaned back in my seat, taking her all in. I could tell I was making her uncomfortable because she was fidgeting and shit. She quickly snatched the cup and poured her some Henn.

When she lifted the glass, I watched as her plump lips covered the top, and she threw it back with ease. She had the sexiest pair of lips, and man I could see them wrapped around my dick. Sun poured another shot and threw it back slamming the glass on the table. She let out a frustrated sigh and ran her hands through her matted curls.

"How the fuck you end up with Diego?" I had to ask to

take my mind off the other shit I was thinking about doing to her.

She shrugged her shoulders, and then her eyes got misty all over again.

"Fucking Mocha!" she spat. This sounded interesting, so I leaned on the table.

"The fuck she do?"

"I still don't fucking know. I honestly don't even know her that well. I moved to Cali and answered her damn ad for a roommate. Shit was cool, and I never had an issue the whole nine months I was there. I don't know what she got herself into, but this nigga shows up to snatch her and grabbed me on GP." She shrugged.

"She must've owed that nigga some money, and you don't want to owe him. Speaking of which, you cost me twenty grand tonight," I told her.

All she did was shake her head.

"Well, I don't know what to tell you because I ain't ever seen twenty grand in my life, so I don't know how I'm going to pay you back. At this point, you can just kill me." She sighed.

"Oh, there you go. I was looking for you." Mocha entered the kitchen with a smirk on her face.

One thing about me I could read a motherfucker like a book and Mocha was as fake as they come.

"No, the fuck you wasn't. I don't even know why you're talking to me!" SunJai snapped, and that shit caught me off guard. It had to be the Hennessey.

"Girl, I heard voices and was making sure you were ok. Where was this energy when you were in the ring?" she spat.

"Aye, quit the bullshit! The fuck you doing down here?

It's clear she don't fuck with you from what I done heard," I interrupted. Mocha's face frowned up, but she said nothing.

"Can I fucking help you?" I snapped because my patience was running thin just that fast.

"If you came down here thinking I was about to fuck you because you been giving me the fuck eyes all night, you got me fucked up. You here for one reason and one reason only, and that's to fight until I get rid of your ass!" I barked.

Mocha jumped, and she turned to walk off just as fast. SunJai looked at me, and this bitch smiled.

"I ain't do that shit for you," I told her. I was lying like a motherfucker, but she wouldn't know.

"Can you teach me to fight?" she blurted out then held her head down.

"I was gone teach your ass anyway because Midnight fucked you up. You got winded too quick," I told her. She nodded her head, taking in what I said.

"Thank you," Sun said and poured another shot.

THREE

SUNJAI "SUN" PERKINS

Lord, the last few weeks of my life, had been turned upside down. I didn't know whether I was coming or going. The shit I witnessed while staying out at Diego's was sickening, and I thank God for getting me up out that situation, even though I was still in a shit storm. I moved to Cali with hopes of taking my career in hair and makeup by storm. When I saw an ad for a roommate, as I said, it was perfect.

Mocha and I were on different schedules, so we barely saw each other half the time. Our bills were paid, and there was no issue. When I came home one day and two big ass men were in my living room, I didn't know what to think. There were no words spoken. A bag was just thrown over my head and I was whisked off. There was no one to look for me because my parents were dead, so escaping was something I only dreamed of.

This man Diego was nothing that you wanted to cross. The things he did were like shit you see about in the news or movies. That man had women from damn near everywhere, doing God knows what. The entire time there, I was trying to figure out what the hell Mocha had got me into.

Whatever it was would hopefully explain how she was coming up with money. The only thing that saved me was me telling a lie about being pregnant. I watched how they would place different women in different places. The pregnant women, even though still treated like shit, weren't treated half as bad. I rode that wave until he shipped us off. To leave that place untouched from the foul and filthy men that we saw was a miracle in itself.

When we got here to the new place, I didn't know what the hell I was getting into. When the dude everyone was calling Bossman stepped in the room, I was shook. Not only because I was scared, but he was fine as hell. If you have never seen an African god, he was the epitome of one. His presence was so crucial that when he entered the room, everything ceased. The deepness of his voice was like a slowly beaten drum in tune. The other girls had become a little cliquish, but at this point in all of this, all I had was myself.

When I found out that we had been traded to a damn fight club, I knew I would not survive this shit. I wasn't a fighter. My life was peaceful. Even coming up as a kid, I wasn't one to fight. I wasn't a confrontational person. One thing I picked up on quickly was that I was gone have to have thick skin being here and around these grimy chicks.

After Bossman told us the rules, I had no choice but to fight all I could. Even though I got the hell out, that shit wasn't going to happen anymore. Now, we both were sitting here, and regardless of how he wanted to act, I felt a connection when he spoke up to Mocha. Maybe it was the Hennessey, but I was feeling a little better.

"So, does Bossman have a name?" I asked.

The way he leaned back in his chair was even sexy. One thing about him that really stood out to me was his gold teeth. Usually, it wouldn't be something that would attract me to a man, but the way the gold and his dark chocolate skin combined did something to me.

"Eze," he smirked.

I placed the ice that I had down on the table because it had started to melt. I gently touched my face and winced at the feeling.

"Yeah, you gone have to show Midnight you ain't no hoe because she did you dirty with that," he smirked.

"If I had some makeup, I could cover it up with no problem." I sighed.

"So, you're one of them, huh?"

"One of what?" I answered.

"One of them females that cake they face in makeup when it's clear you don't need it."

"Actually, I don't wear makeup. I'm a lip-gloss and keep my eyebrows shaped up type of female. Makeup and hair are what I moved to California to do. I'm really good at it."

"So you from Cali?" he asked.

"No, I'm from Texas, but I moved to Cali and was only there nine months until all this shit started to happen." I sighed.

Looking around the kitchen, I took in how big it was. I was starting to get sleepy, but I was trying my best to avoid the other girls because we were sharing a room.

"Do you stay here?" I asked.

"Damn, you sho ask a lot of questions!" he snapped.

"I'm sorry. I really was just trying to keep the conversation going so that I wouldn't have to go back to the room. I just know they're probably waiting up to start some shit," I mumbled.

Eze stood up from the table and hovered over me.

"Follow me and bring that bottle," he demanded in a

commanding tone. I got up from the table slowly and grabbed the bottle, following him out of the kitchen.

Following behind him instead of going downstairs to the rooms, we went up the stairs. Walking down the long hall, we came upon a room. Reaching into his pocket, he pulled out a key and unlocked the door. He stepped inside, and I just stood there. I don't know what he had in mind, but I was having impure thoughts, and this wasn't the time for this shit. Lifting his hand, he held out the key.

"You can stay here. You don't have to share a room with them. I normally don't let girls upstairs because Bullet stays on the other end, and when I'm here, this is where I sleep, but I rarely stay here," he told me.

Stepping inside the room, you could tell it was made for a man. I walked inside, and Eze shut the door behind me and locked it. I quickly turned back towards him.

"Girl, chill out, don't nobody want your ass," Eze said and walked over to the couch that sat on the opposite side of the room.

I just stood there as he sat down, then he looked up at me.

"Aw shit." He sighed and got up, walking over to the dresser. He removed some items and laid them on the bed.

"Here goes you something to sleep in, if you want to get comfortable and freshen up. The bathroom is through that door," he said, holding his hand out.

I was confused, so I looked at his hand.

"The Henn, my nigga!" he barked.

I quickly handed him the bottle and grabbed the clothes off the bed, heading to the bathroom. Earlier, when we left the ring, we had to take a three-minute shower downstairs, and I still felt nasty. As soon as I made it in the bathroom, I looked in the mirror and started to cry again. This shit on my face was hideous. Removing my clothing, I turned the hot water on and stepped in the shower.

Closing my eyes, I let the water run over my head and down my body. After standing there for a few minutes, taking it in, I grabbed the soap that was in the shower caddy and squirted it in the rag I had and slowly started to lather my body. The feeling was euphoric, and I didn't even want to get out of the shower. The thoughts that were creeping in my head was fucking with me. All I could think about was Eze out there on the couch and me entering the room with water dripping from my body. I wanted him in the worse way, and I didn't know why. He was a man of mystery, and I just knew he had multiple women he was entertaining. I mean, look at him.

Turning off the water, I stepped out of the shower and grabbed a towel for my hair, wrapping it up. Using the other towel, I dried my body off and threw on the shirt he gave me. I couldn't wait to make some money because I needed some smell good shit. There was no way I was putting on his stuff and heading into the bedroom smelling like a man.

Once I was dressed, I removed the towel and combed through my hair. My curls needed some attention bad due to the lack of care. Looking at myself, I felt somewhat better until I got to the shiner that graced my face. Leaning on the sink, I closed my eyes and said a small prayer.

"Lord, I don't know where I'm at or where I'm going, but I thank you for removing me from the situation I was in. I never question your work, and maybe I'm here for a reason. Please guide me through it so that I can live to tell about it whatever it is." I smiled at the last part.

FOUR

EZE

The entire time SunJai was in the shower, I imagined myself in there with her bending her ass over. This girl had clouded my thoughts, and that was a no-go. A nigga was slipping hard even letting her stay up here and not with the other girls. I had never done no shit like that. I could tell this wasn't for her. This life was something she wasn't built for. She could never handle a nigga like me.

She carried this sensitivity about her that I didn't want to taint. That shit speaks volumes because I never possessed caring feelings for the opposite sex. Blame that shit on my mammy. I ran my hand across the scar that graced my stomach and felt my anger rising. Grabbing the bottle, I took a swig straight from it. The door opened, and SunJai came from the bathroom and took a seat in the bed.

"Thank you. You just don't know how that shower felt. I know you already doing a lot for me by letting me stay in here, but is there any way that I can get some feminine products? I need shampoo and smell goods; you know all the basics. I didn't want to come out here smelling like you, not that you stink or anything."

"Hush," was all I said because she had started to ramble.

Instantly she shut her mouth, and I just stared at her. Damn, she was fine as hell. My dick rocked up so fast that I had to lay my ass back on the couch and turn away from her. This wasn't that, hell no. I could hear movement behind me, which sound like she was getting comfortable in the bed. Looking back over my shoulder, she had snuggled up underneath the blanket and laid out.

"Fuck!" I snapped and got up and headed to the bathroom.

Turning the shower on, I hopped in and tried my best to stroke me out a nut because shorty was all over my mind. I just needed to bust this nut, or I was one minute away from going out there and giving her this work. I started to think of stupid shit while I washed the night's dirt off me. Instantly a nigga started laughing when I thought about ole girl earlier.

After about ten minutes, I got out of the shower and wrapped a towel around my waist. Standing in the mirror, I removed my golds, placing them on the sink so that I could brush my teeth. The ugly ass gash on my stomach would always be seen, and no matter how hard I tried not to look at it, it just stood out like a sore thumb. As soon as those thoughts plagued my mind, I had to shift my thought process, and I be damned if SunJai didn't pop up.

Standing in the door of the bathroom, I looked at her thick frame in the bed. When she sat up and looked at me with lustful eyes, I knew it was on, and she wanted a nigga.

Cutting the light off, I walked towards the bed. *Don't let me regret this shit.* Yanking the cover back, she gasped at my actions. Reaching for her ankles, I pulled her body towards me, placing myself between her legs.

"Take that shit off!" I told her, referring to my shirt she had on.

She quickly pulled the shirt up over her head and tossed it behind her. I knew her body was perfect, and she had the perfect set of breasts. Sizing her up, you could feel the tension between us. What happened next caught me off guard. Sun reached for my towel, making it hit the floor. My dick popped up and sprang in her face like a Jack-in-the-box.

The way she looked at it, I just knew she was scared until she took me in her mouth. See, this shit wasn't supposed to pop off like this. Sun wasn't half bad, she looked innocent, but I knew once I saw them lips of hers, she was a bad motherfucker on the mic. Looking down at my dick playing hide and seek in her mouth, had a nigga's head rolling back. Not too many females could suck my dick right, and I don't know why the fuck they didn't. I guess they were intimidated.

When I placed my eyes back on Sun, she was looking at me seductively as spit dripped from her mouth onto my dick. Slowly she leaned her head to the side and traced her tongue down my length. That was it. Pushing her back on the bed, I opened her legs and glanced down at her thick ass pussy. That shit was glistening. Using my finger, I traced along her lips, letting her juices coat my tips. The moan that escaped her lips let a nigga know she was ready for this dick.

Opening the drawer beside the bed, I reached in to get my rubber. When I didn't feel it, I scooted back and looked inside, and the shit was empty. Fuck, ain't no way I was about to slide up in her raw.

"Come on, fuck me," she moaned, reaching for my dick, trying to put it to her entrance.

"Man, shorty, I ain't got no rubber. I ain't with that raw shit." In my head, I was fighting like a motherfucker because a nigga was so hard, I could've put a hole in the wall.

"Noooo! I promise you I don't have anything. You can pull out. I haven't had sex in over a year, and I need this right now," she begged.

She was really begging for the dick. She reached for my man again, placing it at her entrance. So, I rubbed the head up and down her pussy. She was so wet that I had no choice but to slide in.

Man, no lie. Sun's shit was tight as hell. She was about to get all this work since she asked for it. I pulled out and smacked her leg letting her know to turn around. She got up on all fours and looked back at me flipping her hair over her shoulders. Damn, that shit was sexy as fuck. Her hand came from underneath and started fingering her pussy.

I slid right back in, and we would see if she could take this dick. I was never the type to brag on my size, but I wasn't no little dick nigga, and that I knew for a fact. I never had no complaints about my dick game. I was known to arrange a few organs.

Sun was into it, and if I didn't know any better, she was liking the long strokes from the back because she was creaming everywhere.

"I wanna ride," she moaned, biting her lip. Yeah, she was trying to show out.

I slid out and laid on my back. Sun climbed over me and grabbed my dick, placing it inside of her. She slid down, slowly taking it all in. Knowing she needed time to adjust, I smirked as she continued to slide up and down on my shit. I placed my hands behind my head to let her think I was bored.

SunJai looked down at me and winked. The next thing I knew, she sped up and grabbed her breasts. She started riding the shit out of me. I had to remove my hands from behind my head and place them on her waist. She was taking this dick like a pro. Shorty was a freak.

"You thought I couldn't handle that dick, huh?" she spat, placing her hands on my chest. The next thing I knew, this bitch slid them hoes around my neck. Aw hell no, she was trying to bitch me. She was into that choking shit.

I reached for her hands, and she smacked them. So, I reached up and placed my hands around her neck. Her eyes rolled back into her head, and she started bucking again. Releasing my neck, she dug her nails into my chest.

"Fuckk girl, damn chill the fuck out!" I yelled.

"Choke me!" she cried out.

Damn, I was already choking her ass. I squeezed a little harder, and I felt her pussy muscles clamp down on my shit. When she did that, I met her rhythm, and just seeing how she was reacting that shit turned me on even more. Not too long after, I was nutting all up in her pussy as she was releasing hers as well.

"Fuck, get your crazy ass up!" I spat, shoving her off me. I hopped out of bed and went straight to the bathroom.

"The fuck just happened?" I mumbled.

I ain't ever felt like a bitch when I was fucking. Sun's pussy was so good that she had me feeling used. Pissing into the toilet, I just shook my head because I was fucking flabbergasted. Flushing the toilet, I turned around, and Sun was standing in the door with the towel I had wrapped around her.

"Fuck is you doing? Don't start all that creep shit," I spat, heading to the sink to wash my hands and my dick.

"Sorry if I kind of got carried away," she blushed, biting down into her bottom lip.

"I let you have that. You choke my ass again and your

other eye gone be black," I lied. I had to put my balls back intact let her know I was that nigga.

She shrugged her shoulders, and I walked past her heading back to the bed. I was tired as fuck, and I felt my body crashing. While she was cleaning herself, I climbed underneath the covers and was out like a light.

FIVE
SUNJAI

I got a feeling I put it on Eze too much too soon. I should have eased it on him that I was a freak during sex. No matter what he said, I know I freaked him out. He wasn't expecting that shit from me. My pussy was still throbbing because I still was feeling his shit. That man was blessed beyond measures. I knew I was about to be sore for a couple of days.

Entering the bedroom, I looked over to the couch, and he wasn't there. My eyes zoomed to the bed, and he was knocked out and snoring at that. Sliding underneath the covers, I pulled them close to me and sleep came easy. I felt secure for the first time in a long time just being in Eze's presence.

―――――――

"YO, EZE!" I heard someone yelling. It sounded like his friend.

Opening my eyes, I could hear light snores, and I realized I was lying on his chest, and his arm was draped around me. Looking down at his stomach, I noticed it was a long scar running across. I wondered what happened. Tracing my finger along the scar, I jumped at him grabbing my hand.

"Eze!" Bullet yelled again, and he shot up.

"What nigga?" he called out.

"Check your phone and let me know before I walk off. It's the count." Eze looked at me then shoved me off of him.

"She good?" he called out.

All you could hear was Bullet laughing and walking off. Eze locked eyes with me, and he rubbed his eyes, shaking his head. Giving me his back, he stood up and adjusted his boxers.

"What happened to your stomach?" I had to ask.

"Look, I'm finna tell you now. Last night was just a fuck, so don't start prying into my personal life. Just because you woke up in a nigga's arms, don't let that shit go to your head. You need to get up and get ready and be in the basement for training. I'll be back in a few hours," he said flatly and started to get dressed.

Well, that wasn't expected. I swear this man was hot and cold. To say my feeling weren't hurt, I would be lying. His words were hurtful. Once he got dressed, I was still sitting there in a state of shock, tucking my feelings and my face because I was embarrassed.

"Bullet should be bringing you a bag up here in a minute with some clothes and the other shit you needed," he said and walked out the door.

Throwing myself back onto the bed, I kicked and hit the mattress in frustration. *SunJai, get your shit together and don't let this man get you into a funk. I mean, I should've known just by his looks alone not to expect nothing but hard dick coming from him. Fuck him. I need to focus on getting up out of here.*

Slowly, I pulled myself out of bed and was walking toward the bathroom when there was a knock at the bedroom door. Turning on my heels, I headed to the door. Cracking the door, I saw that it was Bullet. He held up a huge bag.

"Eze said this is for you." He laughed. This nigga always thought shit was funny.

"Thank you," I said, reaching for it.

"My nigga like you. I can see that shit." He nodded before walking away. Closing the door, I shook my head because his nigga had a way of showing shit.

I threw the bag on the bed and opened it. Inside where some Ethika legging sets with the sports bras, Victoria Secret underwear and pajamas, some smell goods, and shampoo. There was no room for complaints when I had nothing. Finding the remote, I turned the TV on and found Pandora. As the music filled the room, I headed to the bathroom to take care of my hygiene.

WHEN I ENTERED the kitchen area, all eyes were on me. The permanent mugs on the other girls' faces were enough to make one hide in the corner.

"Where were you last night?" Mocha spat.

"Somewhere you wanted to be," I replied, grabbing me a bottle of water out the refrigerator.

"Oh bitch, you ain't ever been this vocal. What done got into you?" she had the nerve to ask, and all the other girls started laughing,

"Me, now get y'all asses downstairs and get ready to

glove up!" Eze spat, entering the kitchen. I thought he left. I didn't need him to come save me, and I wasn't going to thank him.

I turned to walk out of the kitchen, and he grabbed me.

"Stop letting them bully you," he had the nerve to say.

"I wasn't letting them do anything. I was perfectly fine in handling them. You came in here putting your two cents in!" I snapped.

"Yeah, well, you need hands to match that smart ass mouth." He laughed. I didn't see shit funny, and I snatched away from him, heading to the basement.

Walking downstairs, I felt Eze walking behind me, and I could tell he was staring a hole in me. Entering the room, I stood off to the side away from Shrek and her crew. Grabbing a ponytail holder, I pulled my hair up into a ball on my head. I started to laugh because all the other girls were straight mugging me. I couldn't help they shit wasn't real or long.

"Yo, eyes over here. Y'all some jealous ass bitches!" Eze spat.

"Jealous of what?" Mocha spoke up.

"Apparently Sun, because all you been doing is picking with her. You're the fucking reason she even here. I can't wait till she knocks your black ass out. Get the fuck on the treadmills!" he shouted.

I just stood there, taking it all in. Eze stood there in some black jogger pants that came to his ankles. The matching jacket he had on fit him snuggly, showcasing his huge arms. Eze walked over to me, and I quickly directed my eyes up to him.

"Come on. I want you on this treadmill. Last night you got winded too fast. When you get tired, you get weak, and it can cause you to lose. While you are on here, I want you to jab this bag until I say stop. Only jab with the right for now," he instructed.

Nodding my head at the instructions, I got up on the treadmill and did what he told me.

"You know how you got all deranged on me last night. Bring that energy to a fight," he whispered. Once the machine started, it was go-time.

SIX

MORIAH "MOCHA" ALBRIGHT

I hated that hoe with everything in me. SunJai was one of them chicks that thought she was the shit because of her looks. I couldn't see why Eze was putting all his focus on her. When SunJai called me in response to my roommate wanted ad, she was cool people, and I figured in due time she would be this impressionable chick. We had no issues while living together. She was gullible, and I was trying to mold her for this dirty world.

My take on survival was different from what she called herself doing. I was already tainted all because of my big daddy Diego. I was Diego's favorite chick. What started as something small and fun for the moment, progressed into me falling in love with him and helping him run his business. The truth was I stayed running roommate ads, eventually stage a kidnapping, and Diego gets the girl in the end. That's what I called myself doing with SunJai, but she pulled a fast one talking bout she was pregnant and shit knowing she wasn't.

I convinced Diego to let me come to Eze's fighting ring because bringing in 20 to 40K a night was faster and easier money. All these hoes were dumb, and I could easily get away with the shit, going back to Diego at any time.

Look at Eze all over there catering to that hoe. I was the best thing he had in here. All I needed to do was put this pussy on him, but nah she had to block my plan from that last night. I was so glad Midnight whooped her ass. You just wait until we get a chance to get in the ring. That pretty little face of hers would be no more.

"I'm sick of this shit. I want to punch something!" I yelled, cutting off the machine. Eze turned around, and he placed the bag he had down and made his way over to me.

"The fuck you just say?"

"I'm tired of this treadmill, and I'm ready to punch some shit," I repeated.

"Do it look like I give a fuck about what you tired of? You in my shit, and you do as I say. Matter of fact, I can send your ass right back to Diego because I don't have time for you and your smart ass mouth. I don't tolerate shit from nobody, and I'm not finna start with bum ass bitches like you!" Eze spat spit flying all in my face. *Oh, he was big mad.*

"No, please, I'm sorry. I swear I won't say anything else to you," I pleaded, trying to squeeze out some fake tears.

"Glove up, get your ass in the ring!" he spat. I quickly got off the treadmill and did what he said. When I looked up and saw him gloving up too, I wanted to die.

"The fuck you finna do, nigga?" Bullet asked, walking up to him.

"I'm finna knock this bitch out. She wanted to punch something, well shit, let's get this shit rocking," Eze had the nerve to say, stepping in the ring.

"Bring your ass, don't get scared now!" he barked, hitting his gloves.

"Nigga, you too damn big to be fighting her. Stop letting

these hoes get in your head. Come on, nigga, now!" Bullet yelled at him.

Eze had changed, he had blacked out, and it was like darkness came over him. He snatched the gloves off and threw them on the mat, jerking away from Bullet.

"Bitch, you lucky!" he barked and walked out the basement.

The other girls looked at me. Even SunJai was wearing a smirk on her face. This shit was far from over, and SunJai better watch her fucking back. I mugged the hell out of her and restarted the treadmill.

SEVEN

BENARD "BULLET" LEE

Eze had lost his damn mind, and I knew why. Being around Eze for the longest, it was known that he had a short fuse. We headed to the man cave, and I pulled out a blunt passing it to him. Nobody knew that Eze and I were blood cousins. Everyone just thought we were homeboys. My father and his mother were brother and sister. We both had different upbringings. Mine somewhat better than his, but I never treated him differently. I knew no matter what he went through at home that he needed somebody in the background no matter the situation.

Eze's mama was a different breed, and honestly, I couldn't tell you what the fuck her problem was, but she hated Eze with a passion and his entire life, she let him know just that. She would beat on him with everything she could get her hands on. She even stabbed him in the stomach, trying to kill him when he was ten. My nigga was fucked up.

"My nigga, what the fuck is up with you? You ain't ever snapped out like that on our workers," I asked. Eze laid back in the chair, taking a hit of the blunt.

"You remember my fifteenth birthday? Yo pops had just copped us them matching outfits and shit. Something was off with mama that night, and she cracked that beer bottle over my head talking bout she wanted to hit something,"

"The first time you hit her ass. Hell yeah, I remember that shit, I thought you were gone die that night she beat you so bad. What the fuck that got to do with you spazzing out back there?" I asked, reaching for the blunt.

"It's already known that I fucked SunJai. I don't know what it is, but I got some type of emotion for her that I don't have for anybody. She's a fucking beast yo in the bed. My nigga, she had me in bitch mode the way she was fucking me last night."

"I figured that much."

"But look, last night, I woke up in the middle of the night and pulled her on my chest. When you came to the door this morning, I damn near tried to break her hand because she was rubbing on my scar. So, you know she asked what happened, and I went off on her. It's like I find myself protecting her from the other girls because that bitch Mocha, she's ill-minded and on some grimy shit. For some reason, I was holding all that shit in from this morning, and then when Mocha got to talking, she reminded me of my mammy, talking bout she wanted to punch something. Like my nigga, you want to keep disrespecting me, and I'm gone show you what the fuck disrespect is," he spat.

Shaking my head, I just looked at Eze like he was crazy.

"So what you gone do? Get this money or send her back to Diego because that shit ain't solved, and she doesn't seem to be the one to bite her tongue. We're trying to make money, not fuck it up. We done came a long way and never had issues with our girls. I know this emotion shit is new to you, and you just met the girl, but you can't let that fuck up everything else. You can't knock out every bitch that tries SunJai scary ass." I shrugged.

"How come I can't, and she ain't scary she just from a different side of the track that's all," he said.

Eze stood up.

"Don't go back in there starting no shit," I told him because I knew he was finna head back down there.

"Man, I'm finna get back to working with Sun."

"Let me find out!" I called out.

Once Eze left, I rolled me another blunt so that I could stay high. That's where my nickname came from. Every time you would see me, the first thing they hollered was, I was bullet as in high. I stayed high. I hated my real name, motherfucking Bernard Lee. My mama had to be sniffing glue when she named me.

At twenty-five, I lived a pretty decent life. Everyone expected me to play ball, but I wanted fast money. When Eze was younger, we noticed his hand skills were lethal, and that's how we made money. Everybody wanted a piece of him and would place bets on fights and shit. We were hurting feelings and emptying pockets. Eze loved to fight for all the wrong reasons, but that was how he released his pain.

I wasn't a fighter, but I could fight. You know Eze had me in the ring plenty times fighting him. The nigga would always say I can't be walking around with a nigga that can't fight.

Fuck all that. I was a shooter and didn't mind pulling my pistol when needed. My motto was to look out for those that looked out for me. Eze and I have had each other back since we were kids. We lived a lavish life, and even now, he didn't have to question my loyalty or where it laid.

There was a knock on the door.

"Yo!" I called out. The door opened, and Midnight

stepped in. She was the house heavy hitter. She was the highest-paid girl we had.

"Hey, boo." She smiled, making her way to me.

Standing before me, she kicked my legs apart, standing in between them. I handed her the blunt, and she inhaled it coming to my face and giving me a shotgun. That shit was sexy as hell. Midnight dropped to her knees and pulled my dick out my joggers. She already knew the deal, no words spoken just a lot of dick choking.

I stood off to the side as Sun and another girl was doing practice jabs. Looking at my watch, they had done enough for today.

"Aite, that's enough for today," I called out.

Sun removed her gloves and placed them back on the shelf. I just stood there watching her, and damn, sweat ain't ever looked so good. Walking over to her, she stopped and looked up at me with those squinty ass eyes.

"You did good today. I see you're a fast learner," I told her.

"Well, I have a good teacher." She smiled. Nope, not falling for that shit.

"Go get cleaned up," was all I said. I can tell she didn't like my response. I had been here way too long. I had to get the hell out of this house.

WALKING INTO MY CRIB, I threw my keys on the table and headed straight to my office. Opening up my laptop, I read over a few e-mails and bookings for upcoming fights. I laughed at the e-mail that popped up next. Shaking my head, I grabbed my phone and placed it on speaker, placing a call. Sitting the phone down on the desk while I continued working.

"My nigga!" the voice beamed through the phone.

"Man, now I'm your nigga. You done got all big time and forgot who the fuck used to knock your ass out back then," I replied.

It was a guy I used to fight in the neighborhood name Sox. Monpre Simmons was a beast with his hands as well. He went legit and opened up a gym called SoxBox Fitness. That shit took off, and he ended up expanding to a few cities.

"You know I ain't forgot where I come from. A nigga's just been busy. You know every now and then I got to check in with you and see if you came to your senses yet." Sox tried his best to get me to go legit, following his steps, but I wasn't ready for that just yet. Hell, I might not ever be ready.

"I hate to deliver bad news, but I ain't ready for you yet." I sighed.

"It's all good, but I ain't gone stop asking. Aye, tho, bring your ass out tonight. I got a section at the club." I could use a little break to go floss a little.

"Let me hit up Bullet, and I'll pull up," I told him.

"Aite bet," he answered, and I hung up.

I shot Bullet a text letting him know the deal. Reaching into my drawer, I pressed a little button I had that opened the safe I had built into my floor. Scooting the chair back that I was sitting in, I removed a stack of money and locked it. Shutting off the computer, I headed to my room to chill until tonight.

Soon as I got in my room, I removed my clothes and laid across the bed in nothing but my boxers. I loved my peace. Just what I needed to reset and get my mind back to where it needed it to be. Today was too much and me trying to juggle that along with my emotions, felt like it was too much for a nigga. No matter what I did, I always tried to block my moms out of my head and life, but since my ways evolved around her, that shit was hard.

She was to blame for why I was a fighter, why I had no respect for women, and why a nigga felt like loving someone was a waste of fucking time. I tried so hard trying to figure out why my moms resented me so much because the shit she would say just didn't add up. When I would ask her why she hated me so much, she would always say I ruined her.

Now, I don't know my father, but from what my mother told me, my daddy was my mama's own cousin. She said he would continuously rape her when she stayed with them, and she got pregnant with me. After she had me, the shit continued, and he ended up giving her AIDS. My mama battled that shit my whole life and was living recklessly with it.

Once I got of age and started having questions of my own, I pleaded for her to see that I was still her child, but she refused to see it. The only thing she saw in me was that nasty ass nigga who impregnated her. A nigga just wanted to be loved and have that motherly figure in my life, but she was disrespectful as hell. I tried for so long to fight the urge to fight her back. I even prayed on it because I couldn't see myself hurting my own mother.

That shit was a different tune when she tried to kill me. This scar I looked at every day on my stomach would never let me forget. Even then, I was too young and just thought mama was sick, and she ain't really mean it. I was like fuck it the older I got. I watch the disease slowly eat away at my mom because she refused to get treatment. Let her tell it, and she'd rather die than raise me. So when she died, I was happy as hell. The fucked-up part was the damage was done, and she had already fucked me up.

That's why this shit was messing with me with how I was feeling about SunJai. No lie, she was like the fucking sunshine a nigga needed a long time ago. It felt like we were opposites, but really, she was sent to a nigga for a reason. I knew I would never be able to give her what she wanted, and that was something steady and probably to be loved. She was out here as well all by herself. We had that shit in common.

Rubbing my hands over my head, I let out a deep sigh. Yeah, tonight was much needed, and I was ready to unwind.

THE SOUND of my phone ringing woke me from my sleep. Grabbing the phone, it was Bullet.

"Yeah," I answered.

"Nigga, you sleep. How you gone invite me somewhere and then not answer the phone?" he asked.

"Man, I was trying to catch up on some sleep, not realizing I was that tired. It ain't gone take me long to get ready. I'll hit you when I'm on the way."

"Aite."

Dropping the phone, I got up and headed to the shower.

Once finished, I headed to my closet. I already knew what I was about to put on. I grabbed a pair of black jeans and a black fitted tee and splashed my body with some cologne. I knew a nigga was finna be the talk of the club tonight, looking at the coat I was about to rock. I had this wheat, black and white pea coat with the wheat fur around the collar, and topped it off with some wheat Timberlands.

Satisfied with how I looked, I headed to the bathroom to brush my hair and clean my mouth and grill. Grabbing my keys, I was out the door.

PULLING UP TO THE CLUB, it was live as hell. I pulled up to valet and hopped out, handing dude my keys. Bullet hit the corner, and we dapped each other up, making our way inside. This shit was live as we made our way through the crowd. I spotted Sox on the upper-level VIP and hit him with the head nod. Tory Lanez "Forever" blasted through the club speakers. I pulled the blunt from behind my ear and lit that bitch up. Bullet started bopping, and I knew he was about to turn up because this was our shit.

"*Aye, my nigga, if you my dog then nigga my dog, we gone get money together. You go through a trial, you ducking the law said fuck it we ducking together!*" I yelled.

"*Shit get wild and you kill a nigga. We bury, shovel together. I got you forever and ever. I got you through every endeavor,*" Bullet followed up.

We got hype as hell on that part. Everybody was looking at us and shit. I blew smoke in some nigga's face and continued our walk through the crowd to upstairs. Once upstairs, my nigga Sox was waiting with a big ass bottle.

"My nigga, wassup?" I yelled over the music.

"Long time no see, you ready to turn this bitch up?" he asked.

"Hell yeah, pop that bottle."

Once the bottle was popped, I grabbed me one and

started to drink straight from the bottle. I spotted one of my little bops in the crowd, and she was eyeing a nigga like a motherfucker. All I did was hit her with a head nod because I knew she was waiting on me to bring her up here, but that wasn't about to happen. It was a few nice pieces up here in the section, and I might just grab one of them because Sox was occupied with his wife, Whyte.

Standing up on the couch, my mind wandered off to SunJai. I should've brought her. She would've had a good time. Lifting the bottle, I took another swig of the hard liquor.

IT WAS ONE A.M., and I was ready to jet. I needed to drop this dick and ASAP. Walking to the exit, I felt somebody pull on my coat. Instantly a nigga was heated because somebody felt the need to touch me. Turning around, I was ready to knock whoever out.

"Eze, you looking for some company tonight?" gal from earlier asked.

"Hell nah, you lucky you ain't looking at the back of my hand because I almost knocked you in your shit for grabbing on me like that," I snapped and jerked away from her.

"I didn't mean to I was just trying to get your attention," she sulked. Giving her the once-over, the dress she had on was fitting her ass like paint.

"Come on, you can suck my dick, dassit," I told her and headed out the door.

I waited on the valet to bring me my car, and she stood beside me like she was the baddest thing walking.

"Meet me round the back in the back parking lot," I told her as I hopped in my car.

I pulled out busting the block coming back round the back parking lot to meet shorty. I don't know what she thought, but I was just about to get this top and dip. Hitting the locks, I let her in and unzipped my pants.

"You want me to do it right here?" she asked.

"The fuck you think? Yeah, I got places to be." I laughed.

She smacked her lips and rolled her eyes, but that didn't stop her from tying that hair back. I leaned back just a little and let her go to work. SunJai popped up in my head again, and this shit with gal wasn't even mediocre. After about five minutes, I could tell she thought she was doing something because she was moaning and shit. Man fuck this shit, I thumped shorty in the ear.

"Aye, I'm good. I got to bounce," I told her, putting my shit back in my pants. I put the car in drive and looked at her.

"What you doing, shorty? Get out," I said, pointing to the door. As soon as her foot hit the pavement, I peeled out.

WALKING INTO THE KITCHEN, a nigga was woozy as hell. I headed straight to the fridge to get me some damn pickle juice. I laughed at the thought that instead of going home, my ass came to the girls' house.

"My nigga, let me find out you about to move in this bitch," Bullet smirked before heading upstairs.

Opening the jar, I took that shit to the head. When I turned around, Mocha was standing there in some skimpy ass shorts and a sports bra. Shorty was fucking dehydrated.

"I just wanted to tell you that I was sorry about earlier. I don't know what came over me," she said.

I placed the jar back in the fridge and closed the door. Walking around the counter, I walked up to her getting in her personal space. Placing one hand on her waist and the other on her head, I used to twirl a piece of her hair around my fingers. Just off me touching her, she was in heaven, and her body was radiating heat like a motherfucker. Leaning in, I got close to her ear and blew it. She placed her arm around me.

"It's something about you that I can't fucking stand. You a grimy ass bitch, and I can't put my finger on it, but your time is coming. You will never, ever, ever get this dick, so you can stop trying," I whispered.

A small gasp came from behind me, and it was SunJai. The look on her face let me know that what she thought she walked in on wasn't what she was seeing. She stormed off, and Mocha started laughing. I pushed her ass in the chair.

"I meant what the fuck I said," I said through gritted teeth.

NINE

SUNJAI

The rest of my day went by smoothly after our training session. All I did was shower and eat good. Most of the night, I kept dozing on and off. When I woke up at midnight to use the bathroom, I couldn't go back to sleep. The sound of a door slamming caught my attention, so I got up and ran to the window. When I saw that it was Eze, I started getting excited. I wasn't stupid, but my first thought was that he was coming to see me this time of night since he doesn't stay here.

Running to the bathroom, I freshened up my breath and decided to go downstairs as if I needed something. Leaving out the room, I made my way down the hall and down the steps. When I hit the corner, I could see the kitchen lights on, so I knew where he was. Easing towards the kitchen, when I turned into the entryway, I felt my heart fall to my feet. Looking at Eze all up on Mocha and damn near kissing her neck sent fire through my body. So lost in my own anger, I let out a small gasp, grabbing the attention of both of them.

Locking eyes with Eze, I turned on my heels and

headed back to the bedroom. Why in the hell was I letting this man get to me? I skipped up the steps two at a time, anxious to get back in my room. Slamming the door, I locked it behind me. What the fuck did he see in her? One minute he was finna knock her head off, and I even told him the mess she put me in, now he's down there trying to get some pussy.

"Hoe ass nigga!" I spat and plopped down on the bed. The bedroom door came flying open, and Eze stood there, shaking his head.

"Damn, that's how you feel about me?" he asked. Rolling my eyes, I faced the TV, ignoring him.

Eze closed the door behind him locking it and started to remove his coat. Tossing it on the couch, I tried not to look at him, but damn, he was fine as hell. Feeling his presence growing near, I was going back and forth in my head with if I wanted to address my feelings. He made it perfectly clear that I was just a fuck.

"Look, what you saw down there wasn't what you think you saw," he mumbled, shocking the hell out of me.

Still focused on the TV, I didn't bother looking his way. Eze grabbed me by the ankles, pulling me towards him, flipping me over.

"What you not gone do is ignore me!" he snapped.

"I don't think it matters if I ignore you or not. You got enough attention from Mocha," I said dryly.

"Not that I need to explain myself to you, but if you must know what happened. My ass was in the kitchen tryna get my electrolytes and shit back up when she came trotting in there half-naked, offering me an apology. You don't think I know she tryna put that wolf pussy on me? I got close enough to get her bothered and told her in so many words that I didn't trust her grimy ass, and soon as I find out what she up to, we gone have a problem. Oh, then I told her she would never ever, ever get this dick." He laughed, grabbing himself. Still, no words left my mouth because I was finding it hard to believe him.

"You don't trust me, Sunshine." He smiled his grill just a gleaming.

"I don't understand you. You don't want me to feel away after the sex we had, but you been doing all this shit since I've been here, giving me mixed signals. Don't call me Sunshine. That's something you have to earn," I told him.

I felt Eze sit down on the bed, and he rubbed his hand over his head.

"Ok, look, I don't know what the hell going on. I think I like you a little. That's why I think I keep looking out for you. I can't give you what you want fully, but I can give you just about everything but this heart, lil baby," he said in a serious tone.

Looking at Eze, I tried to read him, but I could tell by his facial expression that this was a serious moment for him.

"FYI, you would never have to worry about Mocha and me because that hoe reminds me too much of my mammy, and I would kill her." He shrugged.

"Truthfully, I have never met someone that piqued my interests like you. You're so mysterious that I want to know why you are the way you are. Why do you feel you could never give your heart to a woman?" I asked.

"When you give your heart to someone, they have it in their hands and in their control. They pick how they want to break it and when. I loved the fuck out of my mama, but all she wanted to do was kill me. I don't want to leave that pain in the hands of someone else, so I don't get serious with females, and I avoid committed relationships. Plus, you wouldn't be a good fit in my world." Eze sighed.

"If I fight Mocha and win, can I leave?" I asked. There was no point in me trying anymore, so I was going to stop while I was ahead and get the fuck out of here.

"You not ready to fight her, but when you are. You got my word," he told me. That's all I wanted to hear.

I laid back down and pulled the covers over my body and continued to stare at the TV. Eze started to remove his clothes and headed to the bathroom. Once I heard the shower turn on, I closed my eyes and attempted to fall asleep. My nerves were on edge, and I couldn't stop thinking about our conversation. Lifting my head, I punched the pillow a few times so that I could get comfortable. When I heard the water turn off, I closed my eyes and just laid there.

I could hear talking coming from the bathroom, and I knew I wasn't tripping, so I sat up. Looking at the clock, it was late as hell, so I wondered who he was on the phone with. Easing off the bed, I tiptoed to the bathroom getting close to the door.

"Ion need no more girls right now. Nigga, when I do, you need to give me one for free because that hoe Mocha you sent over ass is gone get returned in a body bag if she keeps fucking with me," I heard him say.

I then heard movement towards the door, so I grabbed the handle and pushed the door, pretending I was coming in to use the bathroom. Eze and I locked eyes, and I kept on sliding my panties down and sitting on the toilet.

"Can I use the bathroom please," I said with an attitude.

Placing the phone back to his ear, Eze walked on out the bathroom. My ass didn't even have to pee, so I sat there for a few seconds and flushed the toilet. Walking over to the sink, I washed my hands and came out of the bathroom.

Climbing back in the bed, I covered up and closed my

eyes. Feeling the bed shift, I knew he had climbed his big ass in the bed.

"Sunshine, you going to sleep on me?" he whispered in my ear a little too close for comfort. I could smell the fresh mint toothpaste that he brushed his teeth with.

"Eze, I'm tired, and we have done enough talking for the night." I sighed.

When I felt his rough hands slide around my waist and pull me towards him, I knew he wanted some pussy because he was hard as hell.

"SunJai, can I have you, please? You're the only thing I've been thinking about all night." His voice rumbled to my core. That shit shot straight to my pussy. I wanted to cave in to his wants, but this shit was only going to hurt me.

"I thought you would understand why it wouldn't be more by me telling you about parts of me. A nigga's not blind, and you're turning me on with this no shit. I fucks with you Sun, just not how you want me to," he mumbled, nibbling on my earlobe.

When he did that, it was over because that was my spot. My pussy had won the battle over my mind when his hand slid between my legs lifting them up. After he hit me with that side plank slide in it was done deal.

Standing off to the side, I kept my eyes on Midnight and Mocha as they were fucking each other up in the ring. My money was on Midnight tonight. The crowd was yelling each time Midnight's fist connected with Mocha. Midnight drew back, and this time, I swear I heard Mocha's jaw crack upon impact. Blood went flying, and I scooted back some more as Mocha fell out on the mat.

"That's what the fuck I'm talking about!" Bullet yelled.

This nigga was funny as hell. You could tell they'd been fucking around. My eyes drifted to the box to the other girls, and Sun stood over there with her arms crossed and a permanent mug on her face. My little Pitbull was fine as fuck since her face healed up.

Tonight, she was getting in the ring with a newbie. I wanted to test her skills because I had been putting in work with her. The shit was hard with us being around each other because she had pulled back from a nigga. Not that I was fucked up with it, but I knew she was hurting herself more than she thought she was hurting me.

Regardless, I continued to be me around her. She

turned me on in every way possible, and as long as I had her here, I wanted to enjoy her presence. Look at my ass sounding all sappy and shit. I found myself gifting her with shit here and there all that sucker shit. That night when I told her I could give her everything, you might as well say I've been trying.

"You done making googly eyes with your Sunshine?" Bullet asked, bringing me from my thoughts.

"Fuck you, nigga. I just hope a nigga's not about to regret this bet," I lied. Bullet pulled a wad of money out of his pocket.

"My nigga, you? Hell, I'm hoping she wins this shit to because Midnight snuck and told me that she won a little practice round they did the other day." Bullet nodded.

"When the fuck she linked up with Midnight? She's been doing extra shit behind my back, ole sneaky ass girl." I sighed, looking at her making her way to the ring.

"Let me go up here and start this shit." I walked to the center and signaled for Sun and the new girl to step up.

"Aite, I know last time y'all saw Sun she got her ass beat. All I can say now is don't let the pretty face fool y'all niggas this time. She's been learning from the motherfucking best!" I yelled. Sun stepped up beside me, and she was zoned out.

"Don't get winded!" I yelled and moved out the way. When the bell sounded, Sun moved in with arms up and eyes on her target. The new girl threw a punch, and Sun bounced back quickly and returned a right jab connecting to gal face.

"Get that shit," I said through gritted teeth.

I didn't want to show my excitement, so I kept cool. Gal threw two different jabs, neither connecting with Sun. Sun was running circles and tiring out her opponent. Sun shoved the girl with her right hand, and when the girl stumbled to get her groove, Sun's left hand came up hitting her in the face. When gal head went to the right, Sun connected another hit with her right hand. She was stumbling back my way, so I moved out the way and let her lean on the rope. I started to shake my head. Never let your opponent get you on the rope. Once Sun had her where she wanted her, she began raining blows to her lower body. Right when gal was about to fall forward. Sun came in with an underhanded right hook, knocking gal ass out.

"Run me my money!" I yelled to the crowd and whoever had bet against Sun.

Running over to Sun, I grabbed her hand, raising it up. I could tell she was tired. She couldn't even get her excitement together because she was breathing so hard.

"It's hot. I need some air," she panted.

Bullet signaled for Midnight to come get Sun. While they went off and took care of that, I started making my rounds collecting my coins. The fight could've been better, but considering how that first fight went down, she did her thing. When I rounded the corner, I ran into Mocha.

"You lose this next fight, and your ass is dismissed from the house." I laughed. She didn't know who she was fighting, and I wasn't going to tell her.

ELEVEN
SUNJAI

My ass didn't even want to fight tonight, but I had to show this nigga I was ready for Mocha because it was time to get the fuck out of this house. Over the last month, I didn't know what the hell we were doing because I was trying my best to stay in a non-catching feeling mode. After that night, we had sex again, and Eze started doing things — things like buying gifts and trying to have more conversations. This wasn't me, and I wasn't about to be a weak bitch to him because he was confused as hell. It was hard for me to put my feelings to the side because the longer I was in Eze's presence, it was eating away at me.

Even when it came to training, he spent a lot of time with me to help me get better, and I appreciate that. All the girls in the house hated my ass, except Midnight. When she first reached out to let me fight her, I was skeptical at first, but she was one of the good girls. She called me on my bull-shit with Eze as well. She knew how I felt about him.

Tonight I shocked the hell out of myself when I won the fight. The whole time in my head, I kept hearing Eze's different commands that he would yell out during training.

Then I just thought about how close to being out of here I was, and I lost it. I imagined Mocha's head was the girl I was fighting, and it gave me my win.

Once the fight was over, I don't know if it was the excitement or the heat, but I had to get some air. Midnight walked me outside and handed me a bottle of water as I took a seat in the alley.

"It feels so good out here." I sighed in relief.

"How do you feel?" she asked. Looking up at the sky, the night air was frigid, and I would probably get sick with it being winter, but the feeling of me about to pass out was easing up.

"I feel so good. I'm liable to climb that fence and get the hell out of here." I laughed, then my smile faded when I looked up and saw Eze.

Midnight looked over her shoulder, and when she saw that it was him, she headed back inside.

"What do you want?" I asked.

"That shit was wild, yo. You did good as hell. Here," he said, handing me an envelope. Looking at it, I reached for it, opened it up, and a lump the size of a golf ball formed in my throat.

"What, what is this?" I stuttered.

"Your cut for your win, that's twenty thousand dollars, Sunshine," Eze smiled. My eyes damn near bulged out my head.

"Ain't this yours? I owed you from losing the first fight," I asked.

"Nah, you done paid me back, and I got a feeling I'll get that shit back in the long run. You need to start saving your money so that when you leave, you have something you know for when you go back to Cali," he mumbled the last part.

"Thank you, Eze." I smiled, standing up from the crate I walked over to him and hugged him. He didn't hug me back, but I could tell he was just without actually using his hands.

"Tomorrow, instead of training, I want to take you somewhere if that's cool with you." He lifted his thick brow and grinned at me.

"I guess I can let you do that." Using my hand, I started to fan myself.

"The fuck you fanning for? It's cold as hell out here," Eze asked, walking back towards the door. I followed behind him.

"I don't know. I just don't feel good," I admitted.

"Bullet should be ready to take y'all back to the house."

When we got back inside, I headed straight to get my stuff and then walked back outside to wait in the car.

SHOOTING OUT OF MY SLEEP, I jumped out of bed, dashing to the bathroom. I grabbed ahold of my mouth, trying to catch the contents that were spewing up. When I reached the toilet, vomit went flying out. Clutching my stomach, I sat there dry heaving as I had spit everything out. Slowly I pulled myself up and turned the sink on to brush my teeth. My fucking head was spinning like it was last night, so I went back into the room and got back in the bed.

Looking up at the ceiling, I had a feeling I knew exactly what was wrong, but if it was the case, that was even more reason to hurry up and get away from this house and Eze. I felt a tear roll down my face, and I quickly wiped it away. When I heard the bedroom door unlock, I continue to lay there not moving, and he walked over to my side of the bed.

"Why you ain't up and dressed, Sunshine?" he asked, looking down at me. I turned to face him.

"I am up. I just don't feel good. Is there any way you can run me to the drugstore while we're out today?" I asked him.

"Yeah, but if you don't feel good, we don't have to go out. You can just tell me what it is you need, and I got you."

"No, I'm fine," I said quickly. Eze frowned his face up, but I paid it no attention.

I was about to put on my big girl panties and try my hardest not to look or act suspicious, even though this shit was lingering instead of passing by. Tossing the covers back, I got out of bed and started to get ready.

TWELVE
EZE

When I got to the house this morning, a nigga felt guilty as hell coming in here after SunJai. When I left the spot last night after the fight, I end up fucking with one of my old flights. A nigga had a decent time with shorty too. When I left there early this morning, I went home showered and put on some clean clothes. It was obvious now that I was doing shit to keep from hurting SunJai because I felt like I didn't want to flaunt me fucking with other chicks around her. Even though since we weren't sexing any more, she had to know a nigga was out here doing something.

When I got to the house, the smell of breakfast hit a nigga's nose soon as I walked through the door. Rubbing my hands together, a nigga was hungry too. I entered the kitchen to see Mocha and the other girls cooking breakfast, and my mood changed instantly.

"Good morning, Eze," one of the girls spoke.

"Morning," I said dryly.

"We were just making breakfast for everybody to celebrate SunJai's win last night," the other girl spoke, but I was looking at Mocha, who just looked guilty as hell.

"You a goddamn lie. SunJai ain't about to eat nothing y'all put y'all paws on!" I snapped.

Mocha's guilt showed through her silence. She wasn't talking, but I'm sure she had put the other girls up to speaking as if I would believe any bitch that associated themselves with her. Heading out of the kitchen, I went downstairs to the basement where Bullet and Midnight was. Midnight was sitting in his lap.

"What if I was one of the girls?" I spoke up, interrupting their little session.

"Them hoes know wassup," Bullet spoke.

"You came to go on your little date with your Sunshine," he teased. I was finna cuss his little short ass out.

"Shut the fuck up. You reaching like a motherfucker!" I snapped.

"Real shit, boss, it's fine that you like her. Sun is a great girl, and this shit ain't for her, but I think the two of you both need to stop playing and see how things flow."

"I don't need y'all to tell me how to move through my life and personal situations. What the hell make y'all some experts and y'all can't even figure out what the hell y'all got going on," I said.

"My nigga, it ain't nothing to figure out because we like whatever the hell this shit is. We have good sex, no title, and we just chilling." Bullet laughed.

"Whatever, let me head up here," I said, shaking my head and leaving out the basement.

A nigga ran up the steps I was ready to get my day started with Sun. I knew she would be up because she wasn't one for sleeping in. Using the key, I entered her room, and her ass was still in the bed. Walking over to the bed, I didn't want to say anything, but she looked like shit. Her skin was pale, and she just stared at the ceiling. We exchanged a few words, and she told me she didn't feel good, but we were still going out, so I moved out the way and let her get ready.

Taking my seat on the couch, I scrolled through my phone and was checking the news. Something that I often did to stay on top of shit that was happening close or world-wide. Lately, all this shit with human trafficking was all I was seeing. That made me think of Diego. I had a good run with him, but I slick didn't want any ties to him anymore in case this shit go left. I think I was just going to stick with the remainder of the girls that I have since they been doing good in rotation far as fights. He wasn't going to like that shit, but he was going to have to deal with my decision.

When Sun was ready, she stood in front of me looking good as hell in a Nike sweat suit. Her curly hair was braided in two braids going to the back. No matter what she wore, she looked good as hell.

"You ready to ride out?" I asked, standing up. She held her hand out as if she was telling me to lead the way. We headed downstairs and out the door.

We hopped in the truck, and I looked over at her as she laid her head back on the seat. Suddenly, I got pissed off.

"Are you gone be like this all day?" I flat out asked. Sun lifted her head and turned towards me.

"Like what Eze, what are you talking about now?"

"I mean I know you don't feel good, and I hope that's maybe why you're acting like this, but I was taking you out so that we can have some fun and shit do something nice but if you gone be standoffish like you've been every time I try to do something, then maybe we should stay here," I snapped.

"First of all, if I didn't want to go out with you, I would've told you that last night when you asked. This has nothing to do with me being standoffish. I'm pushing how I feel to the side so that I don't ruin whatever it is you have planned. What the fuck is up with you lately? You sho been in your feelings a lot?" She chuckled.

"Hehe, I don't see shit funny," I said sarcastically.

"Oh shit!" Sun gasped and opened the door of the truck fast as hell just as puke went flying everywhere.

"What the fuck, man?" I hopped out, making sure she didn't get shit in my truck.

I placed my hand over my nose as I neared her to reach into the glove box to give her a napkin. She snatched the napkin and wiped her mouth.

"The fuck did you eat? Gone back in there and handle your mouth, and I'll be waiting on you," I told her. Sun hopped out of the car and went back in the house, ole nasty ass.

Walking over to the water hose, I unwrapped it and turned the water on, spraying the spot with water to get that shit out the way. Once it washed down the driveway, I put the hose back and got in the truck turning the heat on.

SunJai emerged from the house, and she made her way down the steps, she looked a little better had a bit more color to her face. She got in the car and smiled at me.

"Let's try this again," she said.

"I'm taking your ass to Walgreens first," I told her and pulled out.

When we hit the interstate, I turned it on NBA Young-boy's "Ranada" and nodded my head to the beat. I was hoping she caught all the shit he was saying in this song. When I peeped over at her, she was nodding her head, looking out the window. I hit the exit and pulled up into Walgreens.

THIRTEEN

SUNJAI

There was no way in hell I knew I was about to throw up in front of Eze. Lord, on top of being embarrassed, I hope that he wasn't thinking shit. I'm so glad that he gave me time to go inside to freshen up because I needed to get my head together. When I came back out of the house, I was ready and about to put some acting skills to work.

Eze could front all he wanted, but I knew he was in his feelings simply because of what he thought I was doing. I wasn't acting like he wanted me to, and he couldn't handle that. Then he had the nerve to play this song, and I was cracking up inside, even though I was blushing at the gesture. He might not be able to tell me directly how he felt about me, but I could catch the small hints, talking about he thinks he was paying over for some love shit and how he was falling in love, and I didn't take him seriously. The audacity of this nigga, at this point, Eze was confusing his damn self.

Pulling up at Walgreen's, I grabbed my purse and headed into the store while he stayed in the car. The first thing I was looking for was some Emetrol so that I could at least control the nausea. Once I grabbed a bottle of that, I went to the other aisle and just stood there, glancing at the many different boxes. Sweat started to form on my head, and I began to get hot. Using my hand to fan myself, I took deep breaths to calm myself down. I ended up grabbing two different boxes and headed to the register.

After checking out, the lady was placing my stuff in the bag.

"Can you give me those boxes so that I can put in my purse, and you can place the other stuff in the bag?" I asked. She handed me the boxes, and I placed them in my purse. Grabbing the bag and my receipt, I balled the receipt up and tossed it in the trash before leaving out the store.

Getting back into the truck, Eze was looking at me.

"You get your shit?" he asked.

"Yep," I said, holding up the bag. This shit in the bag was nothing compared to the real problem.

We pulled off, and I cracked open the ginger ale I had. We stopped in the street as two kids on bicycles crossed the street. Eze smiled and pulled back off once they passed.

"Do you like kids?" I asked.

"I ain't got nothing against them. They don't bother me." He shrugged. That wasn't what I was fishing around for.

Biting my lip out of nervousness, I continued my line of questioning. "Do you see yourself ever having children of your own? Like do you want any?"

"I ain't never really thought about it. That's not some shit that just crosses my mind. My ass is too caught up in my money to even think about raising a child." He sighed. Instantly I felt my mood change.

"What about you, Sunshine? You look like you would be a decent mom."

"I never really planned for it, but if it happens, I will cherish what's mine, and be the best mom I can be," I stated dryly. We came to a stop, and I looked at the area. The building looked abandon, and I prayed like hell it was no fight shit.

"Get out!" Eze called, stepping out the truck.

Opening the door, I got out and closed the door behind me. Placing my hands in my jacket pocket, I walked up and stood beside him.

"What's this?" I asked. Eze rubbed his chin, and this weird smile crept on his face.

"It's a thought," he replied. I swear to God this man could never just say what the hell it was he meant.

"A thought?"

"I've had this building for years just waiting on the right moment to put my thought into motion. I battle with myself a lot about things. I never know when I'm going to just up and do something, so I just prepare myself ahead of time." He nodded, then hawked up some spit and turned his head, letting it out.

"A nigga's been spitting like a motherfucker!" he spat in frustration.

"Well, whatever your thought is, I'm sure it will be great," I reassured him.

We stood there for a couple of more minutes before we headed out.

The rest of the time with Eze was actually a pleasant experience. We had lunch at one of his favorite places. Then we went on a movie date. Seeing a softer side of him was adorable, even though I would keep that thought to myself.

WALKING INTO THE HOUSE, I went straight upstairs to my room. Bullet had left with Eze, so there was no telling what they were about to go do. As soon as I hit the top step, I heard my name being called. I knew it was Midnight. She was skipping up the steps, and I unlocked the door to the room, waiting for her to come in.

"Hey, girl," I spoke. Midnight sat on the couch, and she shook her head, looking at me.

"Why are you looking at me like that?"

"Before you left earlier, I saw you out there in the driveway throwing up and shit. Then I got to thinking about last night after the fight." She stopped talking and pointed at me.

"You pregnant, ain't you?" she blurted out.

My eyes widened as panic etched my face.

"Would you hush. I don't know. I have to take a test."

"Oh my god, what the hell are you going to do if you are?" Throwing my hands up in the air, I flopped down on the couch beside her.

"I'm getting the fuck out of here. I need this fight to be moved up with Mocha and me."

"Bitch, is you stupid. You know for a fact she's a dirty ass player. What if you're pregnant and she punches you in your stomach or some shit? Why don't you just tell Eze and get this shit over with?"

"Eze doesn't have time for children, and I will not be a burden in his life. I'm not going back to Cali, but I'm taking my money and getting the fuck on." I sighed.

"Look, I can't tell you what to do, but just be safe and really think about this. Eze's mouth may say one, thing, but you don't know how he might feel when you actually tell him. Don't take that chance from him," Midnight said, rubbing my back. I thought about everything she said then looked at her.

"Don't you dare tell Bullet either," I quickly told Midnight.

"I won't. Now, what are you waiting on?" she asked, looking towards the bathroom.

It was now or never time to face the music. Reaching into my purse, I pulled out both pregnancy test boxes I had and headed to the bathroom. Removing both tests from the box, I prepped them and sat them on the sink. My nerves were all over the place. While trying to get my pants down, I was shaking like a stripper. Was I really about to be a whole single mother out here? Once situated, I grabbed both sticks, handling my business.

After washing my hands, I stood there looking at both sticks, waiting for my answer. My ass started to pace back and forth in the bathroom.

"Bitch, hurry up!" Midnight called out. I opened the door and was biting the shit out my nails.

"You look at it. I'm scared," I told her pulling her into the bathroom.

Midnight walked over to the sink, and she bent down, looking at both sticks. I was peeking over her shoulders, and she turned around.

"You are with child," she mumbled, and that shit almost threw me back.

Shoving her out the way, I picked up the first stick and sho enough it was positive. When I looked at the other one, it was positive as well. Instantly tears started flowing down my face.

"What the fuck?" I shouted. Midnight came over to me, pulling me in her arms.

"It's going to be ok, Sunshine," she whispered and consoled me.

FOURTEEN

BULLET

Eze and I were headed to dinner to meet with Diego since he was in town. That nigga was a pop-up kind of nigga, but whatever business Eze had with him, I had with him. We knew him, but after Eze breaks this news to him, it was no telling how he was going to react.

We sat at the table waiting on our food to arrive. A nigga was hungrier than a bitch. I reached into the basket and grabbed another breadstick, taking a bite of it.

"Can't take niggas nowhere." Eze laughed.

"This ain't got shit to do with where the fuck you can take me. My ass hungry ain't ate shit since breakfast," I mumbled with a full mouth of bread.

I held my hand in the air signaling for the waitress. Finishing off my drink, I sat the glass down.

"Yes, can I get you something else?"

"Another refill of the Bacardi, please," I told her. She grabbed the glass and walked off.

When Diego was around his presence was felt with his big ass. I knew it was him walking up due to the two big ass niggas the was leading him.

"Ya boy here," I told Eze. Eze didn't even bother looking behind him.

Diego made his way over to the table, and he stood there as if he was waiting for us to stand up and greet him. I kept chewing my food and hit his ass with a slight head nod. Eze took a sip from his glass.

"Amigos, where's the love?" Diego asked, taking his seat.

"Right here in this food?" I replied.

Diego let out a slight chuckle then focused on Eze who was unbothered. I slowly removed my gun from my hip and sat it in my lap.

"Wassup Eze, you ready to make some more money my friend?" Diego quizzed.

"I'm not buying any more girls from you, so you have to find another way to lighten your load," Eze said coolly.

I glanced over at Diego who wore a shocked expression.

"You mean to tell me you cutting ties just like that with all of the money we made with each other?" Diego responded.

"When I conduct business, I always go with my gut, and my gut is telling me something ain't sitting right, so I'm removing myself."

"You know far too much about my business, so there is no way you are walking away just like that!" Diego hit the table. I clutched my gun and looked at Eze.

"I'm walking away the way I want to walk away. One thing about me I don't take threats or whatever you call yourself doing too lightly. So regardless of what you say, I'm done doing business with you," Eze shrugged.

"What is it that you need? You want girls for a lower price? You name it, and I can accommodate," Diego pleaded. This nigga was not taking Eze serious.

"I don't want anything from you. Our conversation here

is done though," he smirked and picked up his fork and continued to eat his food.

The waitress had been done brought our shit out, but I couldn't eat because I needed to stay ready in case some shit popped off. Once I saw Diego get up and pick his face up off the table, I started to fuck up the plate in front of me.

"You think that nigga is gone come with some bullshit?" I asked Eze.

"Real shit, I feel he already done came with some. I just don't know what it is." Eze shrugged. Just like that, I knew we were about to run into some shit, but we were prepared whatever it was.

FIFTEEN

SUNJAI

It had been a few days since I found out I was carrying Eze's child. The headspace that I was in wasn't a good one, but I was looking out for the life I had in me. I continued to punch the bag and work on my breathing techniques since no one was down here in the basement. Eze didn't know, but I was finna push this fight so that it could happen sooner rather than later.

"Right jab, left jab, duck," I repeated as I did the moves to the bag. I was pumped up and had blocked out everything.

For the next five minutes, I was in my zone. Feeling the bag move away from me caused me to stumble and almost fall. When I looked up, Eze was standing there with a mischievous grin on his face.

"What's got into you?" he asked. Laughing at his choice of words, I couldn't help but laugh at the irony of the question.

"Nothing, I want to fight this weekend for my release," I blurted out. My statement I knew caught Eze off guard because I knew he wasn't expecting that.

"You won one fight and think you ready for Mocha?"

"I'm more than ready for her, and it's not because I won one fight. I have to get out of here like yesterday because I have to take care of something." I sighed.

Something about the way Eze's eyes changed scared me.

"You can just leave. You don't have to fight." He shrugged.

I know I didn't hear him right. If this was the case, I was about to fight him myself if I knew it was that easy.

"Nah, that wasn't the deal, plus I want to win the money because I-I need it," I stuttered.

"Why all of a sudden you need this money and need to leave? What is it that you got to take care of?"

"Can I fight or not?" I blew out in frustration.

"I don't care what you do?" he spat.

"I only have one rule. No body shots or immediate disqualification," I stated even though I was making this shit look suspicious as hell.

"You know it ain't no rules, baby girl." He laughed and walked off.

Fuck! Maybe I should just leave instead of going through with this. Defeated, I sat down on the bench and ran my hands through my hair. Leaning my head on the wall, I placed my hands on my flat ass stomach. There was something inside of me that I had to protect whether I was protecting it from this cruel world or even its own father.

"What's going on with you, Sun?" Bullet voice came hitting me as he rounded the stairs. I bet Eze sent his ass down here for some information.

"What your boy tell you?" I asked him. Bullet laughed. The nigga was always laughing.

"That nigga ain't tell me shit. I'm just asking. You down here going in. I've been watching you on the cameras," he smirked. That was a first. I didn't even know cameras were down here.

"I just need to get away from Eze. My feelings for him are starting to take a toll on me. If he doesn't want to admit to me how he feels about me, then I'm gone," I lied just a bit, knowing whatever I told Bullet, I knew he was going to tell Eze.

Knowing Eze wasn't about to express his feelings to me no time soon that would buy me time to win this fight and catch the first flight out this bitch to Atlanta.

"Well, in that case, I can't even tell you what to do because that nigga ain't finna stop you from leaving. That nigga's pride is a motherfucker."

Midnight walked in the basement and wrapped her arms around Bullet waist.

"What y'all down here talking about?" she asked.

"Why Eze's in his feelings because Sun's ready to leave," Bullet laughed.

"Oh really," Midnight replied, looking at me. She was making me uncomfortable as hell because I knew she knew my secret.

"Yeah, I'm ready to fight, Mocha." Midnight was seriously against this fight since I was pregnant.

"Let me holla at Sun for a minute, baby," Midnight told Bullet and came over to me, taking a seat. Bullet shrugged his shoulders, and we both watched him go upstairs.

Once we heard the door close, Midnight stood up and looked at the top of the steps to make sure he was gone.

"SunJai, what the hell are you thinking about taking this fight?" she snapped going in.

"Don't act like this is brand new to you. I told you I was doing this shit. This is my decision."

"Ok, smart ass, since you thinking and shit, have you

thought about yeah you might win the fight but what you gone do if you lose the baby?" she spat, pointing to her head.

"I asked Eze could he make one rule for no body shots."

"Really? You know it ain't no rules when it comes to them fights. Mocha has it out for you, so you know she not finna half ass this fight. She about to pull everything imaginable just to make you look bad in front of Eze," Midnight said, making perfect sense.

There was silence in the room, as I thought about this shit once again. Mocha wasn't fucking invincible. She just needs to be brought down a few notches. That's when it hit me.

"I got an idea," I grinned. Midnight crossed her arms, looking at me.

"You have to help me, though. Ok, so we never know who we about to fight until they call us, right? What if we can slip something like some Citrate or laxative into her smoothie that she drinks before the fights. She will never think anything about it. Give her that shit before we head out so that about time we get up to fight that shit will hit her during the fight. She will be weak, and as you said, she would do anything in front of Eze to make her feel good and that means even continuing with the fight. All I need is two good face shots, and I can take her down." I shrugged.

"It's possible that it could work, but you don't know how her mind operates. You never know if she will try you below the neck or your ribs. You're still putting your baby at risk," Midnight voiced her concern.

"All I can do at this point is hope for the best because I'm going through with it. So, are you gone help me or not?" All I needed was an answer.

"You know I will help you. I can't wait for this baby to get here so that I can tell him or her how you played with their life." She laughed. Midnight came and sat beside me and placed her hands on my stomach. I placed my hands on top of hers.

"I just hate that Eze will miss out on all of this?" I sighed.

"He doesn't have to Sun, and you know that. Just tell that man and then leave. Like I said, give him that chance."

"I decided I'm going to go to Atlanta instead of Cali."

"Atlanta, that's where I'm from. Why Atlanta?"

"Because it's close to you guys, I think I will feel somewhat safe that I'm still close to y'all," I admitted.

"Yeah, because I'm going to be in my godchild's life fully." We both laughed.

SIXTEEN

EZE

Placing the blunt to my lips, I inhaled the smoke as I watched what was taking place on the screen. Bullet entered the room, and I was sitting back on the couch in the man cave. When he took a seat and looked at the screen, I felt him looking at me.

"You on some creep shit cuz." He sighed, shaking his head.

"Fuck you!" I spat. Grabbing the remote, I aimed it at the TV.

"While you talking, I want you to see something." When I got to the part of the video I wanted Bullet to see, I pressed play.

"So look at the cameras when you walked out the room from Midnight and Sun," I told him. You can see how Midnight looked angry and like she was fussing at Sun.

"Now, I don't know what was said, but you can tell some words are exchanged between them. What the fuck they beefing about?" I quizzed Bullet.

"Shit, they seem cool to me. Sun had just told her about that fight shit."

Bullet seemed unbothered, but this shit was bothering me.

"What's this shit then?" I asked fast-forwarding to another part. You can see Midnight placing her hand on Sun stomach and Sun doing the same.

"Why the fuck she putting her hands on her like that?" Bullet leaned close.

"Nigga, I wasn't there, and I don't know. Frankly, I don't give a damn. Shit, that's that girly shit. You know they be all touchy feely and shit." Bullet laughed.

"You don't care about shit. What if they on that gay shit?" I threw out there.

"What if they are? You ain't making no moves on Sun to let her know that's what you want, and Midnight and me are just on some free shit, so if she wants to bump pussies, she can do her thing." *This dumb ass nigga.*

"What if it's something deeper than that?" I voiced, thinking about what I was about to say next.

"Something deeper like what, Joey Greco?"

"Bullet, nigga, stop playing." I laughed.

"I'm saying you act like a camera crew is about to pull up in a van and hop out."

"What if Sun's pregnant? That day we went out, she was all sick and shit throwing up. Now suddenly she wants this fight and cash because she got something to take care of. Then on top of that, she asks me to make a rule for the fight asking for no body shots, plus that shit right there," I snapped, pointing to the TV. Bullet started to nod his head.

"Hold up, that means you raw dogged shawty? On God, my nigga, tell me you didn't?" Bullet stood up.

I just sat there not even answering that nigga. This nigga bust out in the Bobby Schmurder dance.

"My nigga finna be a daddy!" he sang.

"This shit is serious, not to mention her ass even asked me how I felt about kids and shit and did I ever want any?" I barked. Now, I was getting pissed because she was fucking foul.

"Just ask her and see what she says?"

"I'm gone ask her, but you know what if she goes through with this fight and leave without telling me she pregnant. It's a wrap on her ass forreal. She's probably trying to sneak off and get a fucking abortion."

"So you want the kid but not her?" Bullet asked.

"Hell yeah, I want my fucking kid! I knew what the fuck could happen when I didn't pull out. Regardless of if I want her or not, this shit is foul," I said, getting up off the couch.

"The thing is you want Sun too, so you might as well tell her and y'all raise shawty together. Y'all communication skills all fucked up. Calm down before you go talk to her. You know how you get," Bullet said.

"Aite, Dr. Phil," I blew out in frustration.

———

A NIGGA HAD to leave and go get my dick wet. This shit had me stressed out, and the only way to relieve my stress was to bust a nut. It was late as hell, and I knew her ass would be in here sleep. I crept in the bedroom and looked at the bed, but Sun wasn't there. Panic begin to set in, so I turned around and was about to head downstairs until I saw her coming up the steps with some crackers and ginger ale. *Pregnant ass.*

"Whew, you scared me," she had the nerve to say walking past me.

"I bet I did. We need to talk though," I told her.

Sun placed her things beside the bed on the nightstand and climbed in bed. I just stood there burning a hole in her with my arms crossed.

"Okayyy," she said, giving me this funky ass neck roll. My temper was already trying to show its head, so I counted to ten in my head.

"Are you pregnant, Sunshine?" I just asked, paying attention to her body language.

"The fuck no," she responded way too fast for my liking.

"You wouldn't lie to me about no shit like that, would ya? I just know you ain't on no fuck shit like that?" I spat, hoping to get under her skin to pull the truth out.

"Eze, I'm not pregnant. I've just been dealing with this damn stomach bug. If it makes you feel any better I been shitting up a storm too." She laughed, causing me to frown up.

"So why was Midnight rubbing all on your stomach and shit? I got cameras in this bitch Sun, and I feel you really trying to play me!" I yelled.

Sun hopped up out that bed so fast and got in my face.

"No, no, no sir that's what we not finna do. Me, play you and for what? You the one need to take that damn mask off you got on with all these clown ass games you playing. One minute you this person, then the next you that. You say a lot of things but none of it equates to the coward you really are. Out here fucking all these different women so that your fucking feelings don't get hurt all because your mommy hurt yours!" she spat.

I instantly grabbed her ass around the neck. I wasn't choking her, but she had me fucked up.

"A coward, you really fix your mouth to say that shit. You don't know shit!" I spat. Sun kneed my ass in the dick causing me to let her neck go and grab my dick.

"Then got the nerve to come in here smelling like a bitch that wear cheap ass Bombshell spray. I'm so glad I stopped fucking you, God knows I fucked up letting you hit raw. To answer your fucking question, no the fuck I ain't pregnant. Thank God!" she cried.

"You just in your feelings because a nigga won't be with you," I struggled to say.

"Say what you want, Eze. The more that I'm around you I'm fucking glad you won't be with me. If I was pregnant I wouldn't even tell you because there is no way I would want to bring a child in your fucked-up world. You warned me and told me you were tainted, so you don't need me or no fucking child to taint even further. I mean look at the shit you do. You fucking tied to a man that fucking traffics girls then you try to make it seem like what you doing ain't as bad. Yeah, you might put money in these girls' pockets, but you still harboring them and fighting them like dogs to feed your pockets. You gone do that shit the rest of your life? Nigga, please!" She laughed and walked off.

Real shit, I didn't even know Sun had the balls to even speak to me the way she did. I don't care what she fucking said her feelings were wrapped up all in a nigga. The sad thing she had mine, and that's the only reason I allowed her ass to even go lay down and sleep peacefully.

If she wanted to walk away from me then oh well she can go. I ain't with keeping a bitch that don't want to be kept. Something in my heart told me she was pregnant though, and I didn't care what she said.

SEVENTEEN

SUNJAI

The weekend was here and the only thing on my mind was
the fight. Eze was still walking around here mad at the
world. At first, I felt bad for not telling him the truth when
he asked about the baby, but he had me fucked up, then I
was crushed when he came in smelling just like a female. If
it hadn't of been for Bullet telling me I was fighting, I probably wouldn't have known. Midnight walked in the kitchen
with a sinister grin on her face. The other girls were cooped
up in their room.

"Why are you looking like that?" I asked, taking a bite of
my sandwich.

"Because I'm about to do some foul shit and I need you
on watch," she whispered, reaching into her bag. Slowly she
gave me a glimpse of what she had. I could tell that it was
something in a small box.

"Go watch out over there at the door, and make sure
don't nobody come in here," she demanded.

I stood up from the table and made my way to the entry
way. Midnight opened the refrigerator and grabbed Mocha
smoothie bottle. When Mocha made smoothies in the morn-

ing, she always made enough to have in the evening. Midnight poured the entire bottle in Mocha bottle and shook it up. Lord this shit was about to be funny as hell. I placed my hand up to my mouth to hold my laughter in. Once Midnight finished, she placed the drink back in the refrigerator and I went back and sat down.

"You nervous?" Midnight asked.

"Not really. I don't want to go in doubting myself. Hell, if I can keep up with you, I feel I can get the best of Mocha. I'm just ready to leave more than anything. I saw a side of Eze that I didn't want to see." I sighed.

"You told that nigga he had mommy issues. Hell, I probably would've yoked your ass up too. You do know she tried to kill him, right?" Midnight asked.

"Not to sound heartless, but I don't care. He wants to put all his problems on his mama, but he's causing more problems than a little bit walking around here like being in love is the plague. If anything, what he should be doing is trying to be everything but his mama. Ok, your mama dogged you out. She got her karma in the long run, but don't go punishing everybody else because of that."

"True, I understand what you're saying, but I'm telling you now, this shit gone hit the fan when and if he finds out you hid this child after he even asked you was you pregnant," Midnight said.

"Midnight, I don't care. Now, I'm about to take my pregnant ass up here and start getting ready for tonight. I'll see you at the ring,"

I smiled getting up from the table and walking off. I wasn't trying to be rude, but I was honestly tired of the entire situation my decision was made and it is what it is.

When I was walking out the kitchen, I bumped into Mocha.

"Damn bitch!" she spat.

Lord knows I would've loved to smack fire from her. Tilting my head slightly, I just looked at her and smiled.

"Why the fuck you got that goofy ass look on your face? I swear you one weird, bitch!" she spat, bumping me.

"Eze, don't think so," I called out and kept walking to my room. Now, I was itching even more to beat her ass.

EIGHTEEN
EZE

Tonight was fight night, and I was trying my best not to let Sun cross my mind. Her foul ass couldn't say shit to me if she wanted to. She had me so fucked up after that slick shit she let come out her mouth. She wanted to play, well then tonight I was going to make sure she was off her A-game when she got here to fight.

"So this what gets all your time, huh?" Lisa asked.

Lisa was this little piece I had fucked a few times, and her shit was A1 and almost better than Sunshine. I never bring a bitch to where I make my bread but tonight was different. I needed her for a distraction.

Bullet walked over to me.

"The fuck is this?" he asked right in front of shorty. He didn't care if she heard him or not.

"This my little friend Lisa." I smiled. All Bullet did was shake his head.

"The girls are about to walk in. Heads up, I don't know what's wrong with Mocha, but she was looking a little pink on the way over here," he told me.

"The fuck you mean looking a little pink? She ain't that damn light," I joked.

"Nigga, she looked sick as hell. There go your girl," this nigga said all loud in front of Lisa. She couldn't say shit anyway. She ain't know what I had going on or what I was trying to do.

SunJai walked in her and Midnight was in deep convo. She ain't even notice me watching her. All the girls were headed to the back where we kept them until the fight.

"Come with me, baby," I told Lisa.

Leading the way, I headed to the back room with Lisa on my tail and Bullet right beside me. When we entered the room, all talking ceased. SunJai and I locked eyes. I leaned against the table and pulled Lisa in between my legs. Midnight busted out laughing.

"Bullet, get your girl dog," I mumbled.

"He ain't getting shit. He don't run me!" Midnight spat.

Sun started laughing, and when she looked at me, the mug she gave me was deadly. She placed her arms across her stomach, and I peeped that shit. I think she was toying with me, or maybe I was seeing shit. When I looked at Mocha, she was hunched over in the corner looking exactly like Bullet said, sick as hell.

"Well, the first fight tonight was to be Sunshine. I mean SunJai and Mocha."

"You were right. You miss your Sunshine." Midnight chuckled.

"Midnight, shut the fuck up before I fine your goofy ass. I don't know what the fuck done got into you tonight!" I spat. She was pissing me off. I knew she was doing that shit on behalf of SunJai.

"I don't care about a fine. You're in here trying to disrespect my girl with that goofball ass bitch in between your legs. Put that hoe in the ring, and I bet she folds!" Midnight spat. Bullet walked over to her and whispered something in her ear.

"Yeah, check your hoe mayne and that's five G's, my nigga!" I barked.

"I got her fine," Sun spoke up.

"Baby, I know she ain't talking about me?" Lisa's bougie ass spoke.

"Just hush, lil baby," I told her.

"You not fighting tonight since Mocha don't look good," I told Sun.

"Hell nah, this little shit, ain't nothing. I can knock her ass out, sick or not," Mocha stood up wiping her face.

"You would do anything to keep me here. I don't know why. I know you tired of looking at me like I'm tired of looking at you." Sun rolled her eyes.

"Aww, trouble in paradise," Mocha spoke up.

"Fine then, if you feel you can fight, you got it, but this is your warning, Mocha. You lose this fight, and you won't be returning to the house tonight at all. You up outta here. Take your ass back to Diego!" I spat. SunJai crossed her arms and looked at Mocha.

"One rule though, no body shots since Mocha already look like she about to tip over and for other known reasons!" I spat, mugging SunJai looking at her up and down. I grabbed Lisa's hand, and led her out of the room. When I got to Sun, I stopped and looked her in the eyes.

"Good luck out there." I laughed.

"Fuck you!" she spat.

"I already did."

"From what I remember, I fucked you and had you whimpering like a bitch." She laughed.

Bullet grabbed my ass so fast because he already knew. We walked back out towards the ring.

"Nigga, you birthed a monster." He laughed.

"Sun keeps fucking trying me with that slick ass mouth, bruh,"

"Is that why you brought me here, to make your little hoe mad?" Lisa jumped in.

"First off, don't ever question what the hell I do. That girl ain't no hoe," I said, finding myself defending Sun even after we just spoke each other out.

I walked off and headed to the ring.

"Welcome back. I got something special for y'all tonight. We got the new little beast Sun going up against our fallen soldier Mocha over here. Before we get started and y'all see some shit and go crazy. This fight will be no body shots. So this shall be interesting get your bets in folks!" I yelled and stood off to the side.

NINETEEN

SUNJAI

If I wasn't amped to fight earlier, I was now. Eze really tried to play my ass something awful tonight in front of his plastic ass Barbie. He was stooping lower and lower with this game he was playing. Each time he's done something, I swear it just helped me slide more out the door. Fuck it, I was already out the door, but now my ass in the yard.

Standing on my side of the ring, I kept my eyes on Mocha, and from the looks of it, this fight wasn't gone last long. She looked like she would shit right here on this mat if she could.

After Eze made his announcement, I made my way to the center of the ring. Mocha walked over to the front of me. She was sweating so hard that you would've thought she had already fought.

"You look like shit, or maybe you got to shit." I laughed.

Mocha's eyes widened, and she swung before the bell even sounded. I bounced back so that her punch wouldn't connect. Eze was yelling at the fact that we had already started.

"Come on, shitty booty. You got to be quicker than that!" I called out.

"You did something!" she yelled and ran to hit me again. With quick feet, I slid to the right, and she stumbled, falling over.

Shaking my head, I just stood there and gave her time to get herself together. When she finally stood back up, she was pissed. With my left hand, I kept it in front of my chest so that I could maneuver in case she tried to get dirty and go lower.

"When you leave this house, I'm gone be riding the fuck out of Eze's dick right along with that bitch over there!" she spat, causing me to look over there to where Eze was standing, and he was all in the bitch ear and rubbing on her. When she pulled his face towards hers to kiss, I lost it. Mocha got my ass good, though, because when I turned to look, her fist connected to my jaw. This hoe snuck a good one in. The bitch knocked some focus back in me.

Shaking that little shit off, I came back, and I let off a quick left jab, and when she went to block, I hit her with a right. Mocha's head went flying back, and she quickly recuperated. When she came back up, I hit her with a left and a right, both connecting. Mocha bent over grabbing her stomach. I guess I knocked a diarrhea pain to her stomach.

"Get up, bitch!" I yelled.

At this time, I wasn't even looking at Mocha again. All I saw was Eze's head on Mocha's body. Everything he had said and done came back to me, and I went wild with all face shots. Mocha could barely stand. I could tell she was fighting with face pain from these licks and her stomach pain from the shits she had. She wasn't even swinging back. This last time, she let out a gut-wrenching scream and leaned forward. When she leaned forward, I used my foot swiping it under her legs, causing her to fall on her back. Once she fell out and looked at me, I hit her one good time dead in the face.

Removing my gloves, I started to walk off, then I stopped and turned back around. When I turned back around, I went back over there and hit her ass again without the gloves.

"That's enough!" Eze yelled, grabbing me.

"Don't fucking touch me!" I jerked away from him and left the ring. Midnight was waiting off to the side, and she followed me back to the room. When we got into the room, she hugged me.

"You did it, bitch! You had me scared at first," she admitted.

"Bitch, I was mad when that hoe snuck me. Eze knew what the fuck he was doing. I think he was trying to throw the damn fight knowing that I would get mad," I spat.

"Well, that shit didn't work. It made you blackout and whoop that hoe ass." She laughed.

"Girl, I ain't gone lie all I saw was Eze head on her body," I laughed. The door opened, and Bullet walked in with a somber look on his face.

"What the fuck he sent you in here to do? I hope you came with her winnings because she won fair and square," Midnight started going off.

"Midnight, shut up, damn. This is for you," Bullet said, handing me an envelope. Reaching the envelope, I opened it and looked at the money.

"It's all there I made sure of it. You free to go," Bullet nodded. It was music to my ears to hear that shit.

"Can you take me to the airport?" I blurted out.

"When tonight?" he asked.

"The sooner, the better. I don't need anything but my cash," I admitted. Bullet nodded his head.

"I got you. Let me see what he wants me to do with Mocha's ass." I nodded and watched him leave the room.

Placing my hands on my head, I smiled because I was free. As much as I would have loved for Eze and me to stay on good terms, we had already hurt each other enough.

TWENTY

BULLET

I was tired of playing the middleman to all this shit. I called Eze on his shit when he brought Lisa up in there because I knew what he was doing. He would never bring a flight to the warehouse. We didn't trust everybody, and that's the last thing we needed was another mad bitch that would run her mouth as soon shit don't go her way.

Midnight was letting that ass have it though, and she just didn't know that I would have gladly paid that fine for her ass. Eze was blood, but he knew when he was wrong. He wanted to keep Sun here so bad that even him trying to reschedule the fight because Mocha had the shits was a dead giveaway. Midnight told me what she put in her smoothie. That shit was wild.

After the fight was over, I headed over to him to grab Sun winnings as I did any other night for the other girls. Lisa was standing off to the side, looking bothered and ready to go. I needed to watch her ass. When I came back out from giving SunJai her money, I wanted to run pass him the fact that she was trying to get to the airport fast as hell. This was maybe his last chance to fix this shit.

Eze was at the front door rapping it up with some regulars that supported us. When I walked up, I tapped him on the arm, letting him know we needed to talk. Eze stepped over towards me.

"Sup, you give her that?" he asked, referring to Sun's winnings.

"Yeah, she took it, but peep this. She wants to leave tonight. She asked me to take her to the airport," I paused and looked at him. Eze's whole face changed, and I could tell by how his jaws were flexing that he was pissed.

"You want to take her to the airport and maybe talk to her? This might be your last time, cuz." I sighed. Eze bit down on his lip then rubbed his chin.

"I'm good, homie. She wants to leave drop her ass off then. I ain't taking her nowhere. Ain't no goodbyes," he grumbled before walking away. I just watched him walk off. Eze would never tell me, but I knew he was hurt.

Mocha had grabbed him, and she was saying something to him, but I couldn't make it out. When she walked off, I walked over to him.

"What she want?" I asked.

"The hoe asked me could she go back to the house. I told her nope. She better call Diego or hop her ass in a Lyft to her destination. I'm sick of these bitches!" he spat and walked back off.

Running my hand over my waves, I let out a deep sigh and headed to get Midnight and Sun. Before I could even get back to the back the both of them were walking out the room.

"Let's roll. You sure you don't need to get anything from the house before we head out here?" I asked. She scanned the room, I knew she was looking for Eze, but he was no longer in sight.

"No, I'm good. I got all my money with me, so I'm ready to go," she answered.

We all headed out of the spot and walked to the car. When we got outside, I saw Eze's other car in the distance. I knew he had to be watching us. *Yeah, nigga, get one last look at your girl before she walks out of your life.*

Once inside the car, I started it up and pulled out.

TWENTY-ONE

SUNJAI

Before we left, I wanted to see Eze one last time, but just as I figured, he would be nowhere to be found. During the ride to the airport, I just sat in the back and stared out the window. I wasn't new to starting in new territory, so this would be a piece of cake for me. I already had everything mapped out to what I needed to do once I touched down. Midnight had written me down a list of places for me to visit far as nice areas to stay in and all that. She gave me a cheap phone to use when I got there until I was able to get one. There was no way I was going to travel without a phone.

The flight from Nashville to Atlanta was thirty minutes. The thing was how soon could I fly out on an available flight. As we pulled up to the airport, Midnight turned around in her seat.

"You sure you want to leave? You can always just start over here. Fuck Eze!" she asked.

"Aye, that's still my cousin why you up there talking about fuck him and shit," Bullet spoke up.

"I'm good, Midnight. I promise," I reassured her. Bullet pulled up in front of the drop-off area.

"Look, wherever you go, be careful forreal, and if you ever need anything, you can call me since it's obvious you won't be calling Eze." He laughed.

"I appreciate this, guys. Bullet, tell your cousin even though I can't fucking stand him, I actually cared about him. Hopefully, he breaks out of those selfish ass ways of his." I smiled.

Opening the door to the car, I got out, and Midnight got out as well. She pulled me in for the tightest hug.

"Take care of that baby, and you better call me with every fucking update. I'm the baby daddy." She laughed.

"Midnight, I trust you with this. Please don't tell him," I begged her.

"I'm not telling his ass shit. He done got on my bad side now." She smacked.

"Bye, girl," I told her and watched her get back in the car. She rolled the window down and waved.

I stood there and waved back as the two of them pulled off. Walking into the airport, I was on my own once again to start over and take this world by storm. Atlanta, here I come.

TWENTY-TWO

MOCHA

My life had gone to shit in just a day's time. Now that I know SunJai's ass had something to do with why the fuck I was hugging the toilet for damn near an hour, she was gone pay, not only for that shit but here I was headed back to fucking Diego.

This shit wasn't in the plan. I even pleaded with Eze to let me come back to the house and have a rematch. This nigga flat out told me no because he said when he first tried to reschedule, I should've taken him up on that offer instead of trying to show out.

One thing about Eze, he had a fucking way with words, but that shit did nothing but turn me on. I was used to being talked to all kinds of ways because Diego was the same way. He was just a little milder because I was his favorite girl. Once he hears that I was no longer in the house, I knew he was gone to blow a gasket. This was supposed to be an easy come up in money, but my ass lost the last two fights, so I wasn't bringing him in shit.

The Lyft I was in pulled up to the airport, and I placed the shades on my face to hide some of the bruises that graced my face. Good thing I had dark skin because they hadn't started to form yet, but my face was sore as hell, so I knew it was coming. I had a total of ten thousand dollars on me, so I was about to get me a ticket back to Diego's main compound.

Dressed in a sweat suit and hat, I entered the airport on a mission. Walking up to the ticket area, I looked off in the distance, and I just knew my eyes weren't deceiving me. Pulling my shades down just a little, I peeked over them bitches to get a clear view. Well, look-a-here. Where the hell did she call herself going? She was standing in the Delta line. I pushed my shades back up and made my way towards her. She was so focused on the screen above her that she didn't even peep when I stood behind her.

She was next in line, and there was a man behind her, which placed him in front of me, so I stood there.

"Yes, I would like a ticket for the next flight out of here to Atlanta, please," she told the lady.

A smirk formed on my face, and I scooted back so that I couldn't be seen and waited for my turn. I guess a little trip to Atlanta would be my next destination.

After she purchased her ticket, SunJai walked off and headed through airport checkpoints. That gave me enough time to get me a ticket to Atlanta as well without her noticing she was being followed. Once I got to Atlanta, I would call Diego and ask for some more resources because why in the hell was she coming to Atlanta and not going back to our home in Cali.

TWENTY-THREE

EZE

It had been a whole week since SunJai left, and I ain't gone front like I ain't been thinking about her. Bullet told me the message she had left for me, and it made me feel a way considering I had time to stop her from even going to the airport, but I wouldn't let that petty shit go. This was my first time stepping foot back in the house since she left, and it didn't even feel the same.

Slowly I made my way up the stairs to my room. Using my key, I unlocked the door and went in. Looking at the bed, it was messy from where Sun clearly climbed out of bed, not making it. The TV was still on. I could even still smell her perfume lingering in the air. Walking through, I walked over to the couch where she had her fresh laundry folded up and sitting there. You can tell she legit left out of here and didn't plan to look back.

I was gone have to call the cleaning lady to come out here and clean out this room and get it back to me and how I had it. I needed to move all Sun's shit out of here.

My bladder was full, so I headed to the bathroom and lifted the seat to piss. Closing my eyes, I tilted my head back as I drained the main vein. Damn, that shit felt good. Finishing up, I flushed the toilet and washed my hands. Grabbing a paper towel, I dried my hands and tossed that shit in the trash. The sight of the trashcan irritated me because it was full as hell.

"This don't make no damn sense!" I spat. Reaching down, I yanked the bag out the trashcan, causing the bag to tear, and the contents went flying everywhere.

"Fuck!" I sighed. I was just gone have to take the whole trash downstairs because the bag had torn.

Grabbing some tissue, I started to pick up the trash when my eyes landed on a stick.

"I know this ain't what the fuck I think it is," I mumbled, getting closer.

Looking at it, it was a pregnancy test. The bitch was positive too. I used the tissue to pick the test up and just stared at this shit. When I looked down, I'll be damned if it wasn't another one. I grabbed that one as well, and it too was positive. Somebody had some explaining to do, and I knew her foul ass was lying to me. I kicked the trashcan over and marched downstairs because I knew Midnight's ass was here.

When I stepped into the basement, she was finishing up a session. When she saw me, she rolled her eyes at me, something she had been doing a lot of. If I knew anybody knew something, I knew it was her ass. Walking over to her, I held the test in her face.

"Care to explain?" I spat.

"What is there to explain, that shit ain't mine," she said, moving around me.

"I know it ain't yours because it was in my bathroom. SunJai was pregnant, wasn't she?"

"I don't know. She ain't tell me if she was," she answered.

"Midnight, don't fucking play with me because this shit serious. SunJai's ass is out there God knows where and with my fucking child. I asked her motherfucking ass to tell me the truth," I ranted.

"You need to calm down. I'm not lying to you. Do you honestly think she would tell me knowing I would tell Bullet and his ass come and tell you?"

"That's your girl, though. I know you would lie for her because you ain't liking me right now," I admitted.

Midnight walked over to me.

"You just trying to find somebody to blame your fuck-up on. You pushed SunJai away, and even when she would've stayed if you had just come to your senses, you pushed her away. That girl out there is about to bring your child into this world, and all she wanted was you to do right. This conversation is needed, but I'm the wrong person to have it with. Now, if I hear from her, I will let her know that you know, and she should contact you other than that I'm just as lost as you."

"I don't believe shit you say. You know exactly where she went. You knew about this baby and everything, and that's why your ass was on camera fussing with her about fighting and rubbing her stomach. Yeah, I saw that shit. You know what, you can get your shit and get out of here as well. You no longer needed here!" I spat, and I meant every fucking word.

"Aye, what's going on?" Bullet came into the room.

"You can help your little girlfriend get her stuff and get out because she no longer stays here," I told Bullet.

"Damn, I knew y'all were mad at each other, but you

about to put the only top hitter you got out now?" Bullet asked.

"Midnight can't make be believe that she ain't know shit about SunJai being pregnant. I bet on everything she knows where the fuck she's at too!" I barked.

"I know nothing about all that, but what I do know is if that is the case that she's out here pregnant somewhere with your seed, then you need to be trying to find her, and Midnight if you know something, you need to tell this man," Bullet said to both of us.

"I told him the truth, but let me get my shit. I can't wait to get up out of here," Midnight sassed.

"Where the fuck you gone go?" Bullet yelled at her.

"Don't worry about it!" she yelled.

Walking off, I looked down at both pregnancy tests and couldn't believe this shit. When I did find Sunshine, she had some explaining to do.

HEY, YOU...YEAH, YOU, FOLLOW DIRECTIONS

If you are a visual reader like me, when you read, you like to connect and feel to the point that you can really see what you're reading as if you're watching a movie. On this page I want you to pretend you're watching a movie, and it's the part where life takes the two main characters in different directions with things like flashbacks and time change. The first thing I want you to do is to listen to this song "3rd 2nd Chance" by Starlito & Don Trip. Link here

https://youtu.be/mgbVOCjytBQ

While this song is playing, I want you to remember the previous chapters the way Eze and SunJai came to meet, their first encounter. Reconnect with the feelings they had with each other. The sexual attraction when they were together. I want you to feel where Eze is coming from with his pain and I want you to feel where SunJai is coming from as well. Think of the good, the bad, and the ugly.

Eze stares off into the night sky, thinking the very things you're thinking. He's thinking about change and the pain he feels. No matter how hard he tried to protect himself from developing feelings for SunJai, they came anyway. Now, there's a child out there without him. Eze isn't in his best mindset now and has become reckless because his head isn't clear.

SunJai purchased a single flower in a porcelain pot when she stopped for food in Atlanta. The flower was pleading for attention and needed nurturing. SunJai stood in the mirror and watched this flower bloom just as she has over the few months she has been here. Not only is she watching this flower bloom, along with her growing belly, but she thinks back to everything she went through with Eze and how she wishes things would have worked out between them. She misses him but is afraid of the outcome once her secret gets out.

Now you can continue to the current state in which time has passed.

TWENTY-FOUR

SUNJAI

Placing the water tin down, I smiled at just how much my flower had grown over the last seven months. When I first moved to Atlanta, I had stopped to get some food from this café, and I noticed the flower. It looked as if it needed some loving, and I did just that. I stayed the first few nights here in a hotel until I found a decent townhouse that was available for me. The money that I had won from the fights was enough to get me settled into my new home, furnish it, and get me a car so that I could get around.

The first month was hectic. I had to return to Texas for a few days to get all the things that I had left in Cali back, such as a new ID, my birth certificate, and social security card. It was like starting over all over again. When I returned to Atlanta, it was time for me to get back to my passion for doing hair and makeup, so I created an IG page and started getting my feet wet.

The clientele here was about the same in LA, but it was faster, and my name had started ringing bells here.

Walking away from the flower, I stood in the mirror and rubbed my hand over my protruding belly. One more month and this girl will be out of me, and I was ready to drop.

"Bitch, did you eat the last of the spaghetti?" Midnight asked, busting into the room.

Midnight told me how she and Eze got into it when I left because she wouldn't break to his questions. So she came back home to Atlanta, and we've been roommates ever since. She and Bullet were still cool, but nobody knew where I had gone, and I wanted to keep it that way. I did always have this eerie feeling over me, and I wasn't sure what it was about, but I tried to brush it off most days.

"Ain't nobody ate that spaghetti, girl. You probably ate that shit last night when you got high." I laughed.

Midnight flopped down on my bed, she had her phone in her hand and was glued to it.

"I got a client in bout an hour," I told her.

"When are you going to stop for your maternity leave because I'm sure them folks get tired of your big ass belly being all in they face?" She laughed.

"I said I was going to work up until I had E'Mani, but that's based on this wedding I'm supposed to do." I shrugged.

"Look at your baby daddy out here living his best life," Midnight said, turning the phone around. Eze didn't have a social media page, but Bullet did, and I looked at the phone. It looked like both of them had a decent time last night. Eze looked good as hell, and after all these months, I still missed him.

"Humph," was all I said and started gathering my things to head to the shop. I rented a booth in an upscale salon to do my business at.

Walking outside, I placed my things in the car. As I closed the trunk, that feeling came over me again. Scanning my surroundings, I looked around to see if I saw anything out of the ordinary, but there was nothing. Shrugging my shoulders, I headed back in the house.

"I'm about to head out for a few hours, so I should be back later. If you need me, hit my line," Midnight said as she was grabbing her purse.

"Aite, girl, I'm about to be right behind you." I sighed and took a seat on the couch for a few seconds.

The bigger I was getting, the quicker my fat ass would get tired just from walking to the car and back. Rubbing my hand, E'Mani was kicking like a motherfucker.

"Little baby, I need you to calm down. You gone be the next Simone Biles, huh?" I laughed at her little active ass.

Looking at my watch, it was about time for me to head out. Atlanta traffic was terrible, and you needed to leave out a certain amount of time so that you couldn't get tied up in it. Before I left, I grabbed me a bottled water out of the kitchen and turned the lights and stuff off. Making sure I had my phone and keys, I headed to the door.

With my purse on my shoulders, I turned around and locked the door. The sound of a gun clicking and being pressed against the back of my head froze me in fear.

"Unlock the door and take your ass back in the house," they said. I instantly unlocked the door, and I was shoved in the house. Tripping over the rug, I caught my fall so that I wouldn't fall on my belly.

"I've been waiting on this fucking day." They laughed. Slowly I turned around to see who the voice belonged to, and my eyes widened in fear.

"It doesn't look like your happy to see me," Mocha laughed. My eyes went from her to between my legs as blood and water were spreading on the floor beneath me.

TWENTY-FIVE
MOCHA

There was no way I was getting gone that easy. That night in the airport, I boarded the same damn plane she got on, and Atlanta had been my new home. Once we got to Atlanta, I called Diego up and explained to him everything that had happened, and we had come up with a plan to help get us back in with Eze. We all knew how Eze felt about his precious Sunshine.

Over the months of following SunJai, I was blessed with an even bigger surprise. This hoe was pregnant. Things were making so much sense now because I knew Eze was the father. I was about to kidnap this bitch again and take her to Diego until she had this baby, then we would put the baby on the market.

This girl came to Atlanta and got on her shit. It reminded me of when we lived in Cali. SunJai wasn't really a bad person, but she thought she couldn't be touched, not to mention she and Eze felt like they could handle me any kind of way.

Today I knew she had an appointment because I was the one to book it under a fake name. So, I waited outside her townhouse until she came out. Once I saw Midnight leave, that was my cue. I knew if she were ever around Midnight, then I would never get her like I had her ass now. She ain't know what hit her ass when I placed this gun to the back of her head.

SunJai finally looked at me, and she realized who I was. A smile graced my face.

"It doesn't look like your happy to see me?" I laughed.

Her eyes diverted to between her legs, and the floor was covered in blood and water. *Shit, this wasn't supposed to happen!*

"Please, you have to call somebody because my baby could be in danger," she cried, holding on to her stomach, then she let out a scream.

"Oh, please, you're probably just in labor." I sighed.

I closed the door behind me and locked it. I had to think fast because now, my initial plan had changed. This hoe wasn't supposed to be going in labor and shit at a time like this.

"Man, are you just going to stand there. I need help," she cried out again, this time reaching into her purse. When I saw she was reaching for her phone, I grabbed it and tossed it at the wall, shattering that bitch.

"No I'm calling the shots, I don't give a damn about you going in labor."

I aimed my gun at her and started looking around the house. Lord, I needed a plan, and I needed one quick because I wasn't sure how long Midnight was going to be gone. SunJai looked terrible, and she was sweating. Her hair was sticking to her face.

"Something might be wrong. This is happening too quickly," she panted, looking down at herself.

I continued to look at her in disgust with the gun still

aimed at her. SunJai slowly struggled to take her tights off, and when she did that, she started feeling around between her legs.

"I'll give you anything, just please call the ambulance. My baby is coming," she begged.

Maybe I could help her deliver the baby then take the baby, leaving SunJai here to die.

"If you try anything funny, I will shoot you, and you won't live to see your kid," I told her in a menacing tone. She quickly nodded her head in agreement.

"What do you need?" I asked.

"Some towels or something I don't know," she panted.

My ass didn't even know where I was going, but I took off through the house looking for the bathroom. I could hear her screams all the way in here, and that shit was fucking with me. Vivid memories of me when I gave birth to my own daughter still haunted me.

I found some towels in the linen closet and rushed back in the living room. When I was headed back that way, I passed the nursey, which stopped me in my tracks. Peeking into the room, it was obvious she was having a girl. The room was beautiful, and it was filled with things. I felt a tear roll down my face and anger filled me. Stomping back out the room, I walked back to her where she laid flat out on the floor out of breath. She wasn't looking good at all.

"Here," I said, throwing the towels at SunJai's feet.

"Oh my god, I think she's coming!" she yelled, placing her hands between her legs.

I bent over and took a peek and had to turn my head. I went back to the room where I found the nursery and grabbed a few items placing them in a diaper bag I saw. Pulling my phone out, I dialed Diego. The phone rang several times until he finally picked up.

"There's been a change of plans. SunJai's fucking having the baby right now. I know I can only get so far. I need your help,"

"She's having the baby now?" he repeated.

"Yes, literally on the floor in the living room." I sighed.

"I'll be at the other compound in Nashville because I have some business to attend to so, once she pops that baby out, get on the road and drive to the outskirts. I will have someone come pick you up from there," he demanded.

"Ok," I said and hung up the phone.

A loud scream followed by a soft cry could be heard from the living room. The time was now, so I pulled my gun out and headed back in there with the diaper bag on my shoulder.

SunJai laid there with blood everywhere, and in her arms laid the smallest baby. She locked eyes with me and saw the bag on my arm. She quickly started to shake her head no. Taking the gun off safety, I held my arm out for the baby.

"Hand me the baby, SunJai," I demanded.

"I'm not giving you my child," she panted weak as hell. Aiming beside her, I let off a bullet in the floor missing on purpose. When she jumped, I grabbed the baby, smacking her with the butt of the gun.

My adrenaline was rushing, and I flew out of the house just as fast as I came in. Running to the car, I hit the locks unlocking the vehicle. My ass didn't even have a fucking car seat, so I tossed the bag in the car, laid the baby across my legs, and pulled off.

TWENTY-SIX

EZE

"Damn, bitch, watch the teeth."

I sighed while I laid here and got some dome. My head fell back as I tried to get in the groove of shit. The other chick that stood in front of me removing her bra, wouldn't take her eyes off of me.

"Get up and let your girl suck it cuz you ain't hitting on shit. Damn, none of y'all hoes can suck dick these days," I mumbled.

A nigga ain't had a decent dick sucking since Sunshine. The way she just popped up in my head pissed me off all over again. A nigga's been hunting for her ass all these months as if she owed me some damn money. The consumption of Hennessey in my body had me doing some wild shit again tonight.

"Lay down and eat her pussy." I stood up and faced them with nothing but my boxers on.

Taking a swig from the bottle I was holding, I couldn't wait to hit both these bitches. They climbed on the bed and started devouring each other in a 69 position. A nigga's dick rocked up so fast.

BOOM! BOOM!

"Eze, my nigga, open up!" Bullet yelled.

The fuck did this nigga want? He knew better to come up in my shit and interrupt my session. I yanked the door opened.

"What the fuck, I'm entertaining nigga!" I spat.

"Aye yo, you need to get dressed, and we need to get to Atlanta fast," he told me. I knew my nigga he was too jittery for my liking,

"What the hell is in Atlanta this time of night, and why are you acting weird and shit?" I asked. Bullet let out a frustrated sigh.

"Midnight called me, and it's Sunshine. Shit is all bad, and we need to get down there ASAP."

"Aww, so Midnight's been with her ass this whole time, which proves that I knew that hoe's been lying for her. Fuck both them!" I spat and turned to walk back into the room.

"Eze, nigga, this shit is serious, and it's time you fucking man up and stop running the fuck away from your problems. Now, I didn't want to tell you everything because I needed you calm, but when I said shit is all bad, I meant that shit. Somebody done took the fucking baby and left her for dead. Midnight is at the hospital with her right now!" Bullet barked.

When those words left his mouth, it was like a piece of my soul escaped my body. That's the lowest shit a motherfucker could do.

"Y'all hoes got to go!" I yelled tossing them they shit while I grabbed my clothes, throwing them on as well.

Man, damn, not my fucking child. I missed everything, and now the kid is fucking missing.

Even though I was mad as hell at Sunshine, I prayed

that she pulled through this shit too. A nigga tossed some money and my gun in a duffle and was ready to bounce.

"We driving or flying?" Bullet asked. This nigga was tripping.

"Nigga, we finna hit this interstate. We don't know when the next flight is leaving out. This shit is critical. Ain't no telling who got my fucking child!" I snapped.

We were out of there and on the road in no time. The drive was silent, but I needed answers.

"Man, what the fuck did Midnight tell you?" I asked. Bullet had a somber look on his face.

"She was all hysterical and was like she came home and found SunJai on the floor in a puddle of blood, and the baby was gone. She wasn't conscious, so she called the ambulance, and they rushed her to the hospital. When they got her there, they were working trying to get her stabilized and shit so that they could get info on her as to who would do some shit like this."

"Midnight's been living with her ass this whole time, lying every time she on the phone with you, and these fools were down the damn street and shit. Sun's selfish ass done kept this whole pregnancy from me. What if I don't get my child back!" I yelled and hit the steering wheel.

"Just try not to think the worse. Just keep in mind that she's suffering to in all this, so please don't get down here and start that blame game shit when both y'all asses been playing games and shit," Bullet said and looked at me.

I just kept looking ahead and didn't even respond.

THREE HOURS and forty-five minutes later, we pulled up at Grady Memorial. Entering the building, a nigga's nerves were so shook. I was about to lay eyes on Sunshine for the first time since she left Nashville. Bullet had already had information from Midnight, so we headed to the floor that Sun was on. Walking towards the room, two officers were leaving out. I hated the motherfucking cops, and I wasn't on my home turf, so I didn't know how these cats got down.

I stood outside the door and said a silent prayer for God to hold my tongue and not flip the fuck out in this hospital.

"Remember what I said, nigga," Bullet mumbled, and I hit him with a head nod. Pushing on the door, I entered the room, and SunJai turned to face me, and then she looked at Midnight.

"I had to call him. I'm sorry." She apologized to SunJai.

"Ain't no need to apologize, even though you should've done that shit a long time ago then maybe we wouldn't be in this predicament!" I spat.

"Niggaaa!" Bullet shoved me.

"Nah Bullet, I thought about it, and I was going to keep my cool, but a nigga is fucked up behind this right now," I said through gritted teeth.

Walking closer to the bed, I took a closer look at SunJai. I could tell that pregnancy did her well. Her plump face was still beautiful, even with the gash above her brow.

"Who the fuck did this to you?" I spat. SunJai blinked, and tears started to form.

"Dammit Sunshine, we wasting time and crying ain't gone cut it right now. What the fuck happened?" I barked, causing her to jump.

"Sun's just getting up, so she hasn't even told me yet," Midnight chimed in.

"It was Mocha. I didn't even know she was down here. I had a client, and I was getting ready to head out right after Midnight left. When I was on the porch locking the door, I felt the gun being placed to the back of my head. I didn't know who it was because I still had my back to them. They demanded I opened the door and go back inside." Sun paused, and I moved closer to the bed.

"Once I unlocked the door, they shoved me so hard I fell, and I was trying to protect my stomach. E'Mani was already moving like hell all day."

"E'Mani, I have a daughter?" I interrupted.

"Yes, so when I finally looked up, I saw that it was Mocha. The girl was deranged, I was in so much pain, and blood and water were everywhere. I sent her to look for some towels, and she was gone for a pretty good minute because I end up having the baby. She came back in there with E'Mani's diaper bag, and she had the gun on me. At first, I refused to give her the baby, then she shot at the floor beside me and hit me with the gun. I don't remember shit after that," Sun cried.

"This bitch got to die on me, bruh," I snapped. Man, I was frustrated as hell, and my face was wet in tears.

TWENTY-SEVEN
SUNJAI

When I awoke in the hospital, I instantly starting asking about my daughter, then I remember that bullshit that happened. Midnight explained to me the scene when she walked into the house. She said she had called my phone and the salon, and I wasn't there, so she flew back to the house. My precious baby, I could still smell her and feel her on my skin. I prayed Mocha had it in her heart not to hurt my child.

Seeing the man I loved standing there after all these months done something to me. Eze was the real situation I didn't want to face just yet, and I knew he was mad, but he was holding it in. To see him cry for our daughter made me feel like shit because I had been selfish and held him from that right.

"Bullet and I are going to step outside for a bit." Midnight kissed my forehead and squeezed my hand. She and Bullet left the room, leaving Eze and me alone with our thoughts.

"Do you think I will get her back?" I asked.

Eze turned to look at me, and he didn't say a thing. He

just burned a hole in me. He was making me feel smaller than smaller.

"Why when I asked you to tell me the truth you didn't?" he whispered, leaning forward in his chair.

"At first you were so adamant about not being with me, I was hurt. It was like things between us had got real rocky, so I was looking out for my child. I know you remember everything I said to you, and I meant that. You told me yourself you didn't want to taint me, so why would I want my child around that. I want my child to experience love and stability. All the things that you hated and that your mom did to you, it's like you had your mind set up that this is my life. It's set in stone and that's it. I don't even know what it is she did that fucked you up,"

"Sunshine, none of that matters, do you not get that? You took it upon yourself to determine whether I get to know my child for your own selfish reasons. I knew when I fucked you raw that your ass might get pregnant, and that wouldn't have been something that I regretted. That's why I came to you and asked. That's why I put Midnight's ass out and why I was out here looking for you because E'Mani is half of me, and I deserve to be in her life. She might have been that one person that I do love besides her selfish ass mammy." Eze mumbled the last part, but I heard it.

"Did you just say you loved me?" I asked.

"It doesn't matter if I said that shit because it doesn't change the fact that I'm still pissed at you. Do you realize had you told me, one your ass wouldn't have been here in Atlanta because I wouldn't have let you out of my sight, and E'Mani would've been here with us instead of out here somewhere?" Eze shook his head and held it down.

"I'm sorry, Eze. I didn't want to fall for you, but I did. I wanted to be the one to help you heal and take away all that pain. I was going to eventually tell you about the baby when I had her, but I did what I thought was right at the time." I sighed.

Eze's phone began to ring, and he answered it immediately.

"Yeah," I watched as his body language changed, and he stood up damn near moving the chair across the room. Bullet and Midnight entered the room, trying to figure out what the problem was.

"Somebody just called his phone. I don't know who it is," I told them. We all watched as Eze pace the floor and whoever was on the other end was talking they ass off.

"Nigga, what the fuck?" Eze yelled. Slowly he pulled the phone away from his ear and looked at it.

"Who was that?" Bullet asked him again.

"Diego. He's got E'Mani," he mumbled.

"Well, what did he say, Eze is my baby ok?" I quickly asked.

"Basically, we got forty-eight hours to get him three million dollars, or he's selling the baby,"

"Well, don't you got it like that?" I asked.

"SunJai, I got money, but baby, I ain't no millionaire just sitting on three million. I need to make some calls. Bullet, roll out with me," Eze said as he walked out of the room.

I looked at Midnight, and there was no way I was going to let this taco-eating ass man get away with selling my child.

"Midnight, I might have an idea," I said.

"A three-million-dollar idea?" she asked, being smart.

"This shit won't cost a dime, but I don't know if it will help or make the situation worse if it backfires."

"Well, what the fuck is it so you can tell Eze?"

"I can't tell him. Now when we were moved around, I

remember details and places at least when we got to Nash-ville. I know where his Nashville compound is. What if I place a call to the police putting them on to a sex trafficking ring? Tell them how I was kidnapped in California and brought all the way here to Nashville."

Midnight looked at me, nodding her head.

"I'm usually not down for the snitching shit, but my god baby's life on the line. That shit just might work. Plus, if Mocha took the baby, she couldn't possibly gone that far, and she sho as hell ain't on no plane with that baby since the police done plastered this shit all over the news.

"Give me that card over there on that table. The detec-tives left it for me in case I remembered anything," I told Midnight. Midnight got the card and handed it to me along with the phone.

Glancing down at the car, I looked over the detective's name, and it was his cell phone.

"Time is ticking, hurry up before they bring they asses back in here!" Midnight spat. Quickly I dialed the number, and the detective answered immediately.

"Yes, this is SunJai Perkins, you just left here not too long ago. Well, I have some more information, and I think I might know who took my child."

TWENTY-EIGHT
MOCHA

The baby and I had made it back to Nashville. I had never been so nervous in my life. She was so tiny, and I knew she was hungry. Thank God for the ride that Diego sent they had some formula, so I was able to feed her and clothed her. She was so beautiful, and I didn't want to let her out of my sight. I almost felt bad for taking her from her mammy, but SunJai deserved that shit.

She and I were in the room. I had just wiped her down and gave her a bottle when Diego's loud ass came barging in.

"Mocha, don't get attached to that baby. I have a huge bid on her going, and it keeps growing!" he barked.

"Nobody is getting attached, but someone does have to watch it. She is tiny, so it's critical for her right now. Nobody wants to buy a baby that's not healthy. You should know that, Diego." I sighed.

"Whatever, you heard what I said. I told Eze they have forty-eight hours to get me three million. No way will that happen since he eased up on his fights!" he roared.

All I did was roll my eyes.

"Ok, well, I'm going to get some sleep while the baby is down," I said, hoping he would get the picture and get out.

Diego left out, and I looked back down at the baby, rubbing her hair. Diego knew exactly what he was saying when he told me not to get attached. At one point, I was pregnant by him. My baby was the only thing I had to look forward to. When I gave birth to my daughter, it was the happiest moment of my life. She was everything I could ask for. My happiness was short-lived when Diego snatched her from my arms and sold her.

Right then, I should've left here, but the money was too good and I had already had nothing once he took her. SunJai's daughter reminded me of just that. Diego was seriously sick that he would give up his own flesh and blood so easy. Somewhere out, there was my four-year-old daughter, and I hoped she was happy. I hoped she knew that I loved her and didn't want to give her up.

Laying back on the bed, I pulled the baby beside me when Diego again busted in the room.

"Mocha, get downstairs and smooth over the new girls!" he barked.

Sighing, I looked at the baby because I didn't want to leave her alone.

"Now, Mocha!" he barked, and I quickly hurried out the bed.

Grabbing a few pillows, I placed a barricade around her since she was still sleeping. I was going to make this quick because I didn't trust to leave her alone. My dumb ass was thinking so fast about hurting SunJai, not realizing my own pain. I wanted her to feel what I felt, but now I didn't want to relive losing another baby all over again.

TWENTY-NINE
EZE

SunJai was discharged from the hospital despite doctors' orders recommending she not leave yet, but we had to get back to Nashville. There was no time to waste, and the clock was ticking. SunJai and I boarded a flight back while Midnight and Bullet drove the car we came down in. SunJai looked stressed staring blanked out at nothing in particular.

"Excuse me, can I get a Jack and Coke, please?" I asked the flight attendant.

The flight wasn't long, but I wanted to make sure she was comfortable. This shit was new to me, making sure Sun's feelings were good even though mine was all over the place and hurting like a motherfucker not knowing what may come of my child. The flight attendant came back and handed me a cup.

"Here, drink this?" I told her. Sun looked down at the cup then back at me rolling her eyes.

"What?" I snapped.

"I can't fucking drink. The first thing I'm doing when I see my child is breastfeeding her." She sighed. I shook my head because my ass didn't even think of that and it was an honest mistake.

"My bad for not thinking, I was just trying to take the edge off," I told her before tossing the drink back myself. That shit was hitting too.

"I'm sorry you had to endure that. No woman should have to deal with no shit like that," I said. SunJai didn't say anything.

"What is it that you're trying to do because I'm not used to this nigga here?" SunJai asked, pointing at me up and down. I couldn't do shit but laugh.

"That shit was an eye-opener. What if you would've died or some shit? Like I said, I'm still pissed at you for not telling me, but the reality of it all made a nigga realize how special you are and shit. We gone get E'Mani back, and you won't have to worry about nobody fucking with a hair on either of your bodies," I told her.

"I always thought about you, you know? Whenever I would lay in bed at night, I would wonder if you were with other women. Well, I knew the obvious. If Midnight weren't there, I probably would've broke sooner and called you, but as I said, I felt running away from you was the best thing to do." She shrugged.

"I can see your point now. At first, I couldn't, and you were every bitch in the world whenever I thought about you. You just have to understand that no matter how good of a mother you would've been, a child needs their father. Yeah, a nigga was out here real reckless I ain't got no lie to tell. Hell, when Midnight called Bullet, I was in the middle of finna bang two chicks."

I laughed because she turned her nose up.

"I ain't want to hear all that," she mumbled.

"Now you know I ain't about to sugarcoat nothing, ain't

no point in lying. You know the real reason I was beefing with you though before this baby shit?" I turned to her and asked.

"No, but I know you about to tell me." Sun leaned towards me.

"You told a nigga about himself. The truth hurt like a motherfucker. Like dead ass, I was ready to box your ass. Coming up, in so many ways, Bullet would always tell me the same shit, but it just felt different coming from you."

"So does that mean you gone change your ways? I'm not asking you to be with me because I'm good."

"The fuck you mean you good. You been fucking around when my shorty was inside of you?" I snapped.

SunJai leaned towards the window and gave me a crazy look as if I was serious right now.

"The audacity of you and you were having orgies and shit. Yeah, I ran into this nigga when I first moved there shit got serious," she said, and I clenched my jaw. Nodding my head, I just looked straight ahead before I yoked her ass up.

"Where the fuck was that nigga when you were damn near dead, huh?" I turned to her and spat. A big ass smile formed on her face, and I didn't see a damn thing funny.

"Eze, I was just playing with you boy. Calm down. A nigga was the last thing on my mind when I was there. All I did was work and stay in the house." She shrugged.

"Yeah, aite."

"I'm serious. Unfortunately, I was still stuck on stupid for you."

"I mean, I have that effect on women." Sunshine rolled her eyes at me, and I knew she was sick of my shit.

"You have a daughter now, and I'm sure you don't want her to ever cross a 'you'," she said, and that stung.

"I thought about that because I would kill any nigga that

even looked at her and hurt her feelings. I told myself I was going to give her everything that I ever wanted from my mama."

What shock me next was her sliding her arm into mine.

"What's the story with you two? It's clear you hate her, but I want to know why," she asked.

Looking into Sun's eyes, I could see the sincerity. At that moment, I knew she was hurting due to E'Mani, but she was still wanting to go there with me. It was no point in holding nothing else back, so I told her the entire truth and my fucked up history with my moms.

THIRTY

SUNJAI

After I called the detectives, they came back to the hospital immediately. There was no way I was leaving out anything. I told them all about the kidnapping in Cali, where I was living, and how Diego shipped us here. They did question how I got away, and I explained to them that the girl who hurt me was working with him and she had me out here trying to turn tricks until I beat her ass and ran away. There was no way I was going to throw Eze's name in the mix so I had to fix the story up so that nothing came back to him.

They contacted the Metro Nashville Police and gave them all the information that I had given them about where he might be. I was telling them so much shit, trying to make Diego sound way worse than he already was. I told him he had a big trafficking ring that was spread out in many states, but I only knew of one location. When they told me that they had been trying to find him, but he'd been under the radar, I smiled inside.

I didn't tell Eze that I talked to the police just yet because I knew he wouldn't agree to it. At this point, he had to understand that I would do anything for my child.

As soon as they walked out, Eze came back with Bullet and dragged my ass out of the hospital like Ike did Tina, and we were on the first flight back to Nashville. There was so much on my mind that I wasn't in the most talkative mood, but I was so glad that he broke the silence because our talk brought down walls that I thought would never come down.

When he finished telling me about his mother and all the things she had done to him, I cried like a baby. I had never heard anyone do shit like that to their own flesh and blood. When we finished talking, I just wanted to smother him in love.

As soon as the plane landed, I was anxious to get off. My breasts had started leaking, and my mood changed. I was supposed to be feeding my baby. Only holding her for a few seconds, I would never forget her cry and smell. One of Eze's homeboys had picked us up, and I got in the back seat because they seem to be in an intense conversation.

"Sox, this my baby mama, SunJai," Eze smirked, turning around looking at me.

"I never thought I see the day that my nigga would slip and have a baby." His friend laughed.

"That nigga didn't slip. He knew what he was doing," I mentioned. My mood wasn't the best.

AFTER ABOUT THIRTY MINUTES, we pulled up at a house that I had never been to. Eze got out of the car and opened the back door, letting me out.

"Bullet nem should be pulling up in about another hour. This is my home, and I want you to get comfortable," he said, pointing at my wet shirt.

Covering my breasts, I rolled my eyes and followed him

into the mini-mansion. His place was everything, and I couldn't see why the hell he even had a room at the girls' house because I would never leave this shit.

"Can I get a shirt?" I asked him.

"Why your titties leaking like that?" he frowned.

"It's breast milk, you ass!" I snapped.

"Ok, damn, I ain't know."

"I need my baby here, and I'm starting to freak out because I'm tired of waiting." I sighed as stress came over me.

"As soon as Bullet gets here, we heading to Diego's to see what we can do. If I have to run up in there with guns blazing, then that's what I'm gone do to bring my shawty home."

Hearing him say that made me think if he happened to be there when the police were there. I hated to tell him, but I had to.

"I need to tell you something before you head over there." Eze ran his tongue over his teeth and crossed his arms in his famous stance that he always took.

"What?" he asked in a serious tone.

"Um, when you and Bullet left the hospital, I sort of came up with a plan of my own." I started fidgeting and showcasing my nervousness.

"SunJai, what the fuck you done did?" I stood up straight because I was proud of taking things into my own hands.

"I called the detectives back and told them a little something about Diego and Mocha. I even told them where he houses some of his women here because I remembered the place. I told them how I was kidnapped from Cali, and he has a lot of houses in different states."

"Do you know what you've done?" he yelled.

"Yeah, everything I can to get my child back. I didn't mention anything about you. I'm only telling you this because I don't want y'all going over there and running into them, especially if you going in shooting,"

"We headed over there now, them motherfucking cops should've been there as soon as you fucking called them. I am a man looking for his child. They will understand that shit!" Eze yelled, and Bullet and Midnight came walking in the door.

"They had to get in contact with the cops here first and get the proper shit or whatever they said." I sighed, throwing my hands up.

"You told him?" Midnight asked. Eze turned to her and just shook his head.

"Leave it to Midnight to know everything before my ass. Bruh, let's go!" Eze turned to Bullet and walked out of the house. Midnight walked over to me and pulled me into a hug.

"I had told Bullet on the drive here because I wanted him to be safe. E'Mani will be okay, so go change and I'll be waiting for you," Midnight said, consoling me.

I didn't even know where the hell I was going, but I headed upstairs and starting opening room doors so that I could find Eze's bedroom. The next room I walked into left me speechless. I stood there taking in everything in disbelief.

"Midnight!" I called out to her so that she could hear me. Walking towards the door, I stood there so she could see where to come.

"What you yelling for?" she asked in a worried tone. I pointed to the room, and Midnight came around the corner and walked inside.

"Damn, this nigga's ready." She laughed.

The entire room was a baby nursery. I'm assuming he did unisex colors because he never knew what I was having, but the thought made me feel good that he had prepared for whenever I did come home to introduce him to his child.

THIRTY-ONE

MOCHA

After getting the new girls situated, I was tired and wanted to lie down. Using the key that Diego had given me, I locked the basement door and headed back upstairs. When I reached, the upstairs Diego was sitting in the living area, puffing on one of his nasty cigars.

"Mocha, we need to talk," he said calmly.

"Yessir," I responded, making my way to the front of him.

"You know I'm good at reading people. You should know that by now. There seems to be something bothering me and also something bothering you. As long as we have worked together, you know you have been my special girl. Something's off, and I feel it. I can smell the disloyalty reeking from your pours. What is this that you are holding in?" he asked, taking another puff of the cigar.

"It's nothing, sir, I just have a lot on my mind that's all," I answered because the way this conversation was going was creeping me out.

"I wish I could believe you, no good lying punta!" he

spat, placing his cigar in the ashtray that was on the table beside him. Rage had consumed my body.

"Are you really saying this to me? I can't help that you're creating bullshit in your head. I have always been loyal to you even after you did the worst thing possible to me. I'm still fucking here like an idiot!" I yelled.

"You think I would want you raising an offspring of mine. You're only good for one thing — well, maybe two. Plus, you are far from fit to raise a child. You mad that I sold the baby, but you bring me another one to sell, you crazy bitch. That's a prime example of how foolish you are." He chuckled.

This man had tried me enough, and I was sick of his bullshit.

"Good night, Diego," I said and headed back to the room to check on the baby.

Entering the room, I walked over to the bed and placed my finger under her little nose to see if she was still breathing. She was sleeping so peacefully. Walking over to the diaper bag that I had brought with me, I slowly unzipped it and removed the gun that I had earlier. Diego had told me to get rid of it when I left Atlanta, but I didn't. Clutching the weapon, I looked at the baby and said a silent prayer.

Slowly I walked back out of the room and down the hall with the gun by my side. My mind was made up that I was about to kill this nasty ass nigga. What the fuck else did I have to live for? It was clear I never meant shit to him. How could I be so stupid and allow this motherfucker to manipulate my brain?

Entering the living room, Diego was back sitting on the couch this time engrossed into the television. There was no time for thought and no time for turning back. Diego's phone started ringing, which caused me to place the gun behind my back.

"Hello!" he barked into the phone.

I couldn't make out what was being said, but Diego grabbed the remote and clicked the TV to the cameras. Looking up at the cameras, police surrounded his house. My eyes widened in fear.

"There's no time for that. Make sure the girls get out of there!" he yelled into the phone and quickly turned to face me.

"Why are you standing there like that? The police have the place surrounded. Get to the basement and use the emergency exit to help Brando with the dismissal." He looked back at the cameras, and now several cops had made it to the front door with a ram bar.

"Let's go, bitch!" he yelled, coming towards me. I quickly lifted the gun and hit him twice in the head. Diego hit the floor like a ton of bricks.

Everything from that point on moved slowly, I looked at the camera, and the officers that were on the porch moved back at the sound of the gunfire. That gave me enough time. I knew once I was caught, I was going away for a long time for what I did to SunJai. There was nothing left else for me to do but to end it here and right now. Lifting the gun, I started to shed a few tears.

"God, forgive me," I whispered before I placed the gun in my mouth and pulled the trigger.

THIRTY-TWO

EZE

SunJai had me hot. She knew that shit was messed up. I sat in the passenger side while Sox drove, and Bullet was in the backseat. A nigga was antsy as hell, and I couldn't wait to touch Mocha and Diego. I knew she was a female, but that hoe was about to get knocked the hell out today for this bullshit.

"Say something, my nigga. You ain't said two words since we left the crib," Sox spoke up, breaking the silence.

"I ain't got shit to say," I mumbled.

"Well, nigga, I got something to say, and you gone listen. Yo girl did what any woman would have done. Just like you out here willing to do any and everything to get your child, she did the same, bruh. Whether it was the cops, the fire department, or the next nigga, she set some shit up that will possibly get her child back. It would be different if she ain't warn you or if she threw your name in the mix, and she didn't. She gave them people an entire story without mentioning you. Chill out. That hot head of yours will fuck up a lot of shit if you trying to be with her in the long run.

You got a kid and a grown ass woman that loves your ugly black ass," Sox rambled on.

"He's telling the truth, thug, so let's just calm down and get ready to set this shit off so we can grab E'Mani," Bullet added.

"I just pray like hell she in here. Knowing Diego and Mocha's ass what if they didn't even come here? Like that nigga move around so much."

"Stop thinking the worse." Bullet sighed.

"Yo, ain't this the nigga crib up here with all the police lights?" Sox asked as we drew near to Diego's place. It was dark as hell outside, so I couldn't see the house.

"Hell yeah! Pull behind this car," I told him.

I hopped out of the car and walked in the yard, headed down the driveway with Sox and Bullet following me. These motherfuckers had brought out a SWAT team.

"Hold it right there. You can't come in any closer," an officer approached us, holding his hands to my chest. Looking at his hand, I counted to ten and regained my cool.

"My child is possibly in there, and that's why I'm here,"

"I understand all that but I still can't let you beyond this tape," he said. Right after he finished his sentence, we could hear two gunshots coming from the house.

"Shots fired from within the house. Get them off the porch!" another officer yelled.

My heart was beating so fast I could hear it in my ears.

"We need to get a visual on the inside," I could hear another cop yelling. Then *POP!* Another gunshot came from the house.

"Man, what the fuck is going on?" I yelled.

"I have eyes on the inside. It looks to be two deceased in the living room area. There's no more movement in the house. Send them in now!" the officer on the walkie-talkie ordered.

From where we were standing, we could see the officers use the ram to gain entry into the house. At this point, I was pacing because I was anxious and praying like hell one of them bodies weren't E'Mani. I couldn't take that shit. Ain't no way in hell I could face Sunshine with that bullshit.

"Sir, the house is being searched, and we will let you know something as soon as possible," the officer told me.

When the paramedics pulled up, they rushed into the house. Sox came and stood beside Bullet and I stood on the other side.

"10-4 on the missing kid," I heard the officer on the walkie-talkie tell the officer standing by me.

"10-4, what?" I barked.

Sox patted me on the arm and pointed to the door where a female officer was exiting the house holding something in a yellow tarp looking thing. My heart dropped, and I felt my knees getting weak. I just know my baby wasn't dead.

"Your baby is alive, sir. They found her sleeping." He smiled, and I ran towards the cop.

I pulled that yellow shit off, and she was wrapped in a pink blanket. When I laid eyes on E'Mani, my heart swoll up just like I had imagined. Damn, this was my baby, and I couldn't even tell you how much I loved her before I laid eyes on her, but to hold her in my arms after all this shit had gone down was the best feeling.

"We want to take her straight to the hospital and have her checked out due to the circumstances," the officer told me.

"I'm riding in the ambulance. Let me call her mom and

tell her to meet us," I told her, and she headed to the ambulance.

"Now where the motherfuckers that took her at?" I spat because now I was ready for war.

"There was a male and female deceased inside that matched the description of Diego Hernandez and a Moriah Albright. I'm not supposed to show you these, but it's the least I can do to give the family peace that justice was served. It looked to be a murder-suicide." The officer turned the phone around and I glanced at the pictures. It was indeed Diego and Mocha.

"That's them," I nodded.

"It was about ten women found in the basement as well. Pure fucking scumbag," the officer spat.

"Thank you, officer," I told him. Turning to Sox and Bullet, I voiced, "I'm headed to the hospital."

"I already called Midnight and told her to bring SunJai," Bullet told me.

I didn't even bother responding I ran straight to the ambulance, climbing in the back. The officer was still holding her. She handed me the baby, and I just stared at her, finally taking in her features in the light.

She had curly hair like Sun and them slanted ass eyes. I knew she would eventually darken up because I was a black ass nigga. I could see she had my nose and mouth. It was still too early to tell much, but I couldn't wait until her mommy seen her.

"You gone be daddy's baby girl. I promise to always be here for you and love you unconditionally. You know what I'm gone even love your fathead ass mama for giving me you. Even though she tried to hide you at first," I told her.

E'Mani started moving a little in my arms.

"Yeah, get used to that voice." I smiled. This shit wasn't too bad.

Midnight had given me the best news in my life. We couldn't get to the hospital fast enough. Lord, my baby was safe, and the bastards that hurt me were dead, and I was glad for that shit. It was being reported as a murder-suicide. I didn't know who took whose life, I was just happy my baby still had hers.

Midnight pulled up at the damn ambulance entrance, and I hopped out. We got there so fast, and I think we had beat them. Running into the emergency room, I ran straight to the desk.

"The ambulance was on the way here with my daughter, and I'm not sure if they have made it yet. She's two days old!" I cried. My hormones were out of whack and my breasts were still leaking like crazy.

"No, ma'am, they haven't made it yet," she replied.

I could hear sirens in the distance, so I ran back out the double doors and stood there waiting on them to park. Looking through the doors, when the paramedic opened the door, and I saw Eze, I damn near knocked him over.

"Ma'am, remove your shirt and hop on the bed," the paramedic spoke, and I did what she said.

Once I laid on the stretcher, Eze put E'Mani on my chest and covered her back up. I placed my arms around her and held on for dear life. My tears couldn't stop falling, and I planted a million kisses on the top of her tiny head.

When we got in the hospital, they took us to labor and delivery and did all the testing they were supposed to do, including getting her weight as if I had just delivered her. For her to be born some weeks early, E'Mani weighed six pounds thirteen ounces.

My body was exhausted, and the doctor came in with E'Mani. Eze lifted her out of the bassinet and gave her to me. I wanted her to latch on so she could eat. E'Mani latched on with ease.

"Ms. Perkins, I have to say you are blessed, and your baby is a trooper. God was on her side. Even though born early, she is healthy, and all her tests came back perfect. We checked for signs of trauma and did x-rays to make sure nothing was wrong internally and everything checked out. I do want to keep you guys here a couple of days since I under-stand you had to leave Atlanta suddenly. So, if you have any questions or concerns, you can page the nurse on duty or give me a call. All our info is up there on the board." He smiled.

"Thank you so much," I told him as he left the room. Eze hadn't left my side, and he was just staring down at E'Mani.

"What do you think of her?" I whispered. She was dozing off while sucking on my breasts.

"I think we gone have a problem with her getting the titty more than me," he frowned.

All I could do was shake my head at his stupid ass.

"Nah, forreal though, she's perfect in every way. When they brought her out that house, and I held her, man, it was like I had loved her my whole life. Shit is unexplainable, but we had a little talk, and I had to let her know that her daddy the shit, and I'm going to always be there for the both of you." he smiled.

To hear him talk like that, I knew she had touched him. It was weird but something that I could get used to.

TWO DAYS LATER, the time had come for us to leave the hospital. Everything turned out good for E'Mani and me, so they let us free. I was so glad to be walking up out that hospital and with my child. I was so shaken up with her kidnapping that I kept her in the room with us the entire time. The nursery didn't have to worry about her, fuck that.

Pulling up to Eze's home, I got out of the car while he flew around back to get the baby. It was clear that he still had some areas to learn in how to treat a lady, but I didn't want him to change for me or make it felt like I was changing him. I loved him rough around the edges. With the way he treated E'Mani, I'm sure he would eventually catch on.

He was carrying E'Mani's car seat and talking baby gibberish to her as we walked the steps. Once we entered the house, I sat down fast as hell. Leaning back on the pillow, I closed my eyes for just a second. I could hear Eze on the phone with someone, but I was about to try to get me some rest.

"Aite, I'll be though there in a second," he said, and I whipped my head around fast as hell because where did he think he was going we just got here.

Eze rounded the corner and had the baby in his arms. He leaned forward to hand me her, and I shook my head no.

"I was about to try to get some rest, Eze. So, is this how it's gone be you back out in the streets?" I sighed, grabbing E'Mani.

"Hold up. A nigga still got to eat until I get everything how I need it to be. I know this is sudden, but I promise to make it up to you, and then you can get all the rest you need," he had the nerve to say.

"Eze, I suggest you take the time to spend with us because when we go back to Atlanta, the time apart will be critical."

"The fuck you mean go back to Atlanta? You ain't taking my baby no damn where. You know what we gone talk about this shit when I get back!" he barked and stormed out of the door.

THIRTY-FOUR

EZE

SunJai had a nigga on ten with that bullshit she let fly out of her mouth. The fact that she really thought she was about to go back to Atlanta with my shawty, she had another thing coming. Fatherhood was new to me, and I wanted to experience every aspect of being a father and not popping in and out. The shit about moving back to Atlanta wasn't about to fly with me.

Here I was trying to take steps to do better, and SunJai made me want to go backwards, but at this point, what the fuck was the point? My niggas Sox had called me and told me to meet him at the place. If everything worked out the way I hoped, this would be a good start for me. This was the time to get my mind focused because I had to make this pitch, and this was my only shot. If this shit failed, then it was back to underground boxing for me.

Driving up, I pulled behind Sox truck and got out. Sox stood there with his friend Kasey who was the owner of Black Enterprises. This man specialized in constructing black business and bringing them to the more gentrified factor.

Walking up to Sox and Kasey, I gave Kasey a handshake while dapping up Sox. Looking at the place that I had purchased a long time ago and considered a thought, I was now going to put some action to my thought.

"I don't know if you were aware when you purchased this building that one day this area would be as popular as it is. What type of plan do you have for this?" Kasey asked me.

"I just so happen to train women and some men in fighting and boxing. I want to open a gym for both men and women, but my main focus would be women, as I would start a female professional team of heavyweights and offer self-defense classes for the ladies who done had to deal with a lot of kidnappings and shit, so I think that is very important," I told him.

"Seeing that the next gym and fitness center is a twenty-minute drive away, I think it would be a perfect idea. Just make half deal with boxing and the other half fitness so that you can get more flow instead of catering to one thing," Kasey advised.

"Well, shit, I can do that. Just get me numbers and I'm ready to start."

"Show me around inside, and I will need a copy of the key so that I can have access."

"Shit, let's go." I laughed, and we all headed inside. I watched as he pulled out his iPad and started taking photos.

"I'm proud of you for finally doing this. A nigga was tired of asking when you were going to turn that pain into something. All it took was the right person to bring it up out ya. How's the daddy life treating you?" Sox asked.

I let out a sigh and thought about the shit Sunshine said before I left.

"It's the best feeling. Something that I didn't know I would ever be was somebody's father. Sunshine hit me with some shit today, and I had to hurry up and get up out of there. We had a little spat."

"Damn, already?" Sox asked.

"She wanted to come home and get some rest, but when you called, I had to give her the baby, so she got all mad then started talking crazy like I needed to spend time with them because when she goes back to Atlanta, it will be different."

"Oh damn, I thought you were trying to make it official and shit?"

"A nigga was contemplating that shit, but I know one thing she ain't taking E'Mani motherfucking Sadiq no fucking where!" I barked.

"Look, one thing you gone have to learn when it comes to kids and relationships. Sometimes you got to give and take. I know this meeting was important for you, but real shit, Kasey was gone do the shit anyway. Your child should've come first, bruh. She just came home, and I know SunJai's tired. I would've understood all that. Now the Atlanta shit that's something the both of you gone have to talk about without getting pissed. Being a family man, you have to be understanding. Go home and talk to your girl after you let her get some rest and you tend to your daughter." Sox laughed.

We dapped it up, and I waited for Kasey to come back around before I headed out.

"Aye, let me run something else by you real fast," I told him.

Kasey came over to me, and I explained to him something else I wanted to do as well. Money wasn't an option, and I had plenty of it saved. It was as if a light went off in his head because he started doing some shit on his iPad and smiling hard. He held his hand out for me to shake, and I returned the gesture, sealing the deal.

Heading back out the door, Sox called out to me

"What was that all about?" he asked. I smiled, show-casing my grill.

"Just a little give and take," I told him and headed home to my girl.

I STOOD in my yard and took a toke of the blunt before I headed in the house since I wasn't smoking in the house anymore. I just wanted to be levelheaded when I went inside. A nigga didn't even want to argue though. I just wasn't sure how this shit was going to flow once Sun mentioned leaving again. Like damn, she ain't even consider staying. The shit's been on her mind the entire time.

My phone started to ring, and I reached down into my pocket to pull it out. Looking at the screen, it was nothing but some pussy, so I hit ignore.

I had to laugh at myself for that shit because I thought I would never see the day. Well, we gone see how this conversation goes because I might just have to run that shit back.

Finishing the blunt, I flicked the roach in the bushes and headed in. Upon entering the house, I went straight upstairs because I wanted to get out of these clothes before getting the baby. I ain't want her smelling my loud ass weed.

Walking past the baby room, I heard E'Mani's little mobile playing, so I peeked inside, and she was knocked out. I continued to the room, and I heard the shower running. Removing my clothes, I threw them in the bin and grabbed me some basketball shorts. Flopping on the bed, I grabbed the remote and turned on the TV until SunJai got out of the shower.

THIRTY-FIVE

SUNJAI

Once I laid E'Mani down, I had to hurry up and take a shower. She had only been down for ten minutes, and I was hoping she slept longer since it was night. It was no telling how long Eze's black ass was going to be out, and I wasn't about to call or blow up his phone either.

Stepping out the shower, I heard the TV on, and I knew it wasn't on when I came in here. Wrapping the towel around my body, I grabbed the baby monitor and walked back into the bedroom, where Eze laid stretched out on the bed all into the TV. Placing the monitor on the dresser, I headed back into the bathroom to put this ugly ass pad and panties on before moisturizing my body.

After getting settled, I dreaded going in here, so I slowly dragged myself to the bed and climbed up in it. With my phone in hand, I combed through my IG page and checked a few emails.

"Why are you taking my baby from me?" Eze mumbled, not even looking at me. The sadness in his voice pierced my heart.

"Eze, I'm not taking her from you, but I have a life that I

have to get back to once my six weeks is up, maybe even before then." I sighed.

"Bruh, whatever you were doing in Atlanta, you can do that same shit here. SunJai, we have a child together, and I'm not about to be that father that isn't in the house with her. I'm not missing shit. My life is here, at least the one I'm trying to build. A nigga's trying to do right by you, and I had to step out and handle that today in which I realized after I left I could've pushed it back and been here for you so that you could get some rest. You remember the building I took you to when we went out?" he asked.

"Yeah, what about it?" I asked.

"I'm taking steps, and I honestly want to surprise you, but I can tell you that I ain't doing that underground shit no more."

Hearing Eze say that he stopped the fighting, and that he was working on his dreams made me proud.

"All of that sounds good, but what about me? I just started booming in Atlanta, and now you want me to up and leave that? This was my dream that I was supposed to be pursuing until all this stuff entered my world."

"So, you don't want to make this thing official between us and raise E'Mani in the same household?" Eze asked, and he lifted his back off the headboard.

"Now, you want to make it official?" I asked, lifting my brow. Eze stood up and placed his hands on top of his head. I knew he was mad.

"SunJai, what do you not understand? I'm doing all this shit for you. I told you I loved your ass and all that, and yet you still playing games!" he yelled.

"Hold up. You are doing this for your daughter, not me. You should want this shit for yourself! For me to keep moving around isn't helping what I'm trying to do career-wise." I tried justifying myself. Truthfully, I was scared as hell.

"Sunshine, listen because you're not hearing me. Baby girl, you can do hair and makeup anywhere. Hell, you can have your own fucking studio or whatever you call them shits. Do you know there are traveling makeup artists and stylists? Hell, if you need to go back and forth to Atlanta, then you can do that, but this shit right here that you're trying to pull is exactly what I meant when I talked about a motherfucker having control of your heart.

I told you this was why I didn't love because you got my heart, and now you want to just break it like I don't mean shit to you!" he yelled, smacking his hand with each word. I jumped because E'Mani's cries could be heard through the monitor. I hopped off the bed.

"I got her." He sighed and exited the room.

When he left out, I thought about everything he said. I already had him miss the entire pregnancy, and I knew taking her away would do two things, place us back in a bad space and him going backwards after so much progress forward.

Rubbing my temples, Eze walked back in the bedroom with E'Mani.

"Aye, I think you finna have to pop one of them titties out because she tried to lick a nigga's nipple and shit," he said, handing her off to me.

I couldn't even contain myself I was laughing so hard.

While I got her ready for her feeding, Eze climbed back in bed beside me and just shook his head and looked at the TV.

Was our conversation done or was he done with me?

"We will stay," I blurted out. Eze turned to me, and I nodded my head.

"I'm scared," I admitted.

"What are you scared of? I got you."

"I don't doubt that you do, but this is really your first real relationship. I don't want to be that trial run then when you get tired or it isn't what you think it should be, you up and leave me at the drop of a hat, or even worse you go back through your roster of women." I sighed.

"Sunshine, that's the thing, nobody, and I mean nobody, not nan chick that I ever fucked with got me like you got me. That shit was just physical and nothing more. Can't nobody compare to you, lil baby," he smirked and leaned over, and we shared a kiss. The feeling was full, overflowing, and complete.

EPILOGUE

EZE

Eight Months Later

"Everyone, please welcome your new female heavy-weight champ, Midnight!" I spoke into the crowd, and she started making her way towards the stage.

I was so happy a nigga was beaming. Eze Does Fit was finally up and running. My nigga Kasey had done the unthinkable to this building. A nigga didn't even know it had the magnitude to look this great. On top of opening the gym, I signed two girls, one of them being Midnight. Over the weekend, Midnight competed in her first pay-per-view fight, and she won a title. That was the biggest accomplishment for me besides my business.

Midnight made her way up to the stage and held her belt over her head. Bullet stood off to the side, looking like a proud ass husband. They asses weren't married but they were worse than my Sunshine and me. Sunshine was in the back, engaged in conversation with some woman. Knowing her, she was networking.

If you had asked me months ago if settling down, becoming a family man, and going legit was going to be in my near future for a nigga like Eze Sadiq, I probably would've laughed in your face and cussed you out.

Walking off the stage, I walked around and shook a few hands before heading over to SunJai. She was looking extra spicy today, and I liked the shit. It was something about when she wore the color red. I knew she felt me looking at her because we locked eyes, and she began to blush. After all this time, her ass still blushed as if she ain't have a nigga wrapped around her finger.

"Hey there, handsome, you got a girl?" she asked as she placed her hand on my chest.

"Actually I do, and if she sees me with you, it's gone be an ugly sight," I played along.

"Damn, I was gone show you what that mouth do," she teased.

"Oh, you trying to get me to buy you another building," I joked.

Once SunJai told me that she was staying here, I was glad I told Kasey to make something shake and find a small window front where she could open a salon and makeup studio. Once I showed her the building and told her it was her push gift, she went into diva mode forreal. I was proud of my baby. She was juggling motherhood like a pro as well. We were good for now, and I was happy I could go from giving her that unsteady to steady love from a thug.

SUNJAI

When I tell you, this man amazed me every day he did just that. When I first laid eyes on Eze, I was scared as hell of him, and he was just the meanest. He was someone that I didn't see myself with. Thank God for a black eye and Henny because he's been mine since.

For the longest, he kept me blinded to what he was actually doing with this thought that he had, but when he showed me what he had done, I was proud to say this was my man.

The best part was my push gift. Eze made sure I stuck to my goals and did what I needed to do for my career. Opening my studio up was a good move, and I didn't have to start over. I hired a social media networking team, and the rest is history. Eze wore fatherhood nicely, and he was the best. You wouldn't think that he came up the way he did because he was so perfect with E'Mani. It came naturally to him. I was blessed beyond measures, and I overcame from shit that not all made it out of.

BULLET

"Damn, my girl standing up there looking good as hell," I mumbled.

I smiled displaying all my teeth. I was her number one fan. Now we done had our ups and downs and even still, she wouldn't let me put a title to our shit. She was mine though, and she understood that shit.

A nigga missed the money that I was making with the underground shit, but you know if Eze's eating we all eating. He got me in on this fitness shit, and I was a trainer here at the gym. I had a few young guys that I was working with, coaching them, and getting them ready for the ring.

My eyes landed on a chick that slowly made her way through the crowd. Her eyes were fixed on Midnight, and that shit didn't sit well with me, so I slowly made my way through the crowd, just peeping the scene. As I got closer, I noticed the gun in her hand. She had no clue that I was coming up on her. Pressing the steel in her back, I whispered in her ear.

"You don't want to do that because if you do, then I will

let this motherfucker rip your spine like Jenga. Move with me and play that shit off," I demanded.

Both of us slowly backed away, and I noticed the look of fear on Midnight's face. Once we made it out the crowd, I shoved her ass into the break room, snatching the gun out of her hand.

Eze stepped into the room, followed by SunJai.

"The fuck going on?" he asked.

"That's what I'm trying to figure out. I spotted her in the crowd because she looked off as fuck, so I snuck up on that ass, and she had this gun in her hand like she was about to do something to Midnight!" I spat.

The door flew open, and Midnight stood there with that same look on her face.

"Tera, what are you doing?" she asked her.

"You know this bitch?" Midnight held her head down and let out a defeated sigh.

"Bullet, look, you have to hear me out."

"No, why are you trying to explain anything to him. You have been lying to him for years, and I'm tired. You want to keep playing these games, you lucky he got my gun because I was about to end your happy ass life!" the other chick yelled.

"This sounds like some gay shit, you gay Midnight?" Eze asked with his arms crossed.

"Nigga!" I spat. Midnight never answered.

"Well, damn, bitch is you?" I barked, walking up on her.

"Yes," she cried.

"Now, you want to cry." Tera sighed, rolling her eyes.

"Shit, do what you set out to do then, fuck her!" I spat, handing gal the gun and walking out the room.

I ain't give a fuck if she shot her ass or not out here

playing my ass. Eze and SunJai came behind me, but I didn't stop, I walked straight out of the gym. Fuck these hoes. I was coming to my senses.

The End

THE END

Book two the spin-off of Bullet and Midnight's story coming soon plus more of Eze and SunJai

THANK YOU

Thank you for reading, and I hope you enjoyed this ride, but it isn't quite over. As stated, there will be a spin-off of Bullet and Midnight story, plus I know y'all want some more of Eze and SunJai. The drama hasn't even started yet. Please leave a review good or bad. I love feedback, and I love all of you that take the time to read my work.

KYEATE'S CATALOG